FOREVER LOVE

FOREVER LOVE

R. Jay Berry

TATE PUBLISHING
AND ENTERPRISES, LLC

Published by Tate Publishing & Enterprises, LLC
127 E. Trade Center Terrace | Mustang, Oklahoma 73064 USA
1.888.361.9473 | www.tatepublishing.com

Tate Publishing is committed to excellence in the publishing industry. The company reflects the philosophy established by the founders, based on Psalm 68:11,
"The Lord gave the word and great was the company of those who published it."

Book design copyright © 2016 by Tate Publishing, LLC. All rights reserved.
Cover design by Bill Francis Peralta
Interior design by Gram Telen

Published in the United States of America

ISBN: 978-1-68333-360-9
1. Fiction / Romance / Clean & Wholesome
2. Fiction / Romance / African American
16.05.24

This book is dedicated, above all, to the couples who have been married or have been together for many years yet still experience heart palpitations and increased pulse rates when their significant other walks into a room or love sickness when they are away from them. However, I must dedicate the reason and the writing of this book to my aunt Rheu Dell House, or aunt Rudy as we call her, who personally asked me to write a love story for her to read. She is a true romantic.

Preface

Love truly is a powerful thing. I think it can be said that true love makes you feel and act in certain ways that cannot be explained. I myself still get those palpitations and increased pulse rates when my husband walks into the room or when he smiles at me. I also still hear that bell that I heard the first time I laid eyes on him. After thirty-seven years of marriage, I am still very much in love with my husband. When you think about remarkable love stories, many couples come to mind. Whether these stories are real or just from a writer's imagination, they all have one thing in common: love drives the characters' actions. In most cases, love starts beautifully but ends tragically in death or with lasting repercussions.

The two most notable, most memorable, and most tragic love stories that come to mind were written by William Shakespeare over four hundred years ago—*Romeo and Juliet* and *Antony and Cleopatra*. These love stories were both of two people who could not be together in life for different reasons. However, because they loved each other so much, they found ways to be together in death. Yes, love makes a person do strange things.

Then there were Bonnie and Clyde. How could we forget the crime spree and, yes, love story of this infamous couple? Their love shows us that love does not discriminate against criminals because they too fall in love. The law stopped their reign of crime after two years, but they loved each other until the very end.

True love means the occasional sacrifice. This was indeed the case with the true love story between King Edward VIII and Mrs. Wallis Simpson. For love, King Edward abdicated his throne and monarchy to marry the woman he loved. Though many thought that this marriage would not last, they lived together as husband and wife for over thirty years until Edward's death.

What about those love stories that do not have happy endings? Ever seen or heard of the biographical drama film *Lady Sings the Blues*? It is set in 1928 and is about the life of Billie Holiday, a blues singer, and her true love, Louis McKay. Most people will remember this film mainly because of the stars cast to portray them: Diana Ross (Billie Holiday and Billy Dee Williams (Louis McKay). While there were many notable scenes in the film adaptation, especially her untimely death, the chemistry between the couple—until Billie's death—was undeniable. The one message I got from their love story was that you may not approve of the decisions people make in their lives as they may cause problems for family and friends, but love does not stop in times of trouble or misfortune.

In some cases, true love can also transcend social standing and the lack of wealth. In a movie so aptly called *Love Story*, two people from different backgrounds fell in love. This tearjerker tells the story of a wealthy law student, Oliver Barrett IV, who falls in love with a poor music major, Jennifer Cavilleri. Their love was undeniable, but Oliver's father believed that true love between people with such different backgrounds simply could not happen.

Going even further back in time, there was the sad story of Sir Lancelot, one of the greatest members of the Knights of the Round Table, and Queen Guinevere, who was married to King Arthur. Their momentary stolen moments only resulted in Lancelot becoming and living the remainder of his life a lowly hermit and Guinevere dying a nun. Were those stolen moments worth how their lives ended? I suspect that these lovers would not have traded one moment they had together for their original significantly better circumstances even though they could not be together in the end.

While those mentioned are only a few examples of what individuals are willing to go through for true love, it is important to realize that even in modern times, love knows no bounds. With social standing, ethnic background, economic status, or whatever other reason, true love may not be realized or acted upon. To help explain this very point, we must examine a love story between two individuals: Jeremy Bernard Toliver and Lily Marie Johnson.

1

Our story begins in 1948, with a sixteen-year-old boy named Jeremy Bernard Toliver. Described by his mother as a paper-sack–brown color, Jeremy had a medium build, weighed about 175 pounds, and was 5'11" tall. He had no noticeable outward physical traits that would make him stand out in a crowd, but it was said that he was the spitting image of his father. Because everyone in his family had been given a nickname (or, at least, assigned a shortened version of their name) by their parents, Jeremy had one too. He was called Flutter.

His mother would explain this name by saying, "My baby boy had such long lashes when he was born that when he blinked his eyes, they fluttered like a butterfly's wings." So from the time Jeremy could walk (which was around eight months), the name stuck, and he was called Flutter by everyone in his family.

Flutter was the youngest of three children born to Jacob and Octavia Toliver. Jeremy had two older sisters named Elizabeth (Beth) and Janine (Janie). The couple loved all of their children and had high hopes for them all. However, they discussed on many occasions their concerns regarding their baby boy because he had a hard time making decisions about everything and taking the lead in any situation, and he pretty much did not show any interest in anything.

Octavia often said in her nightly prayers, "Lord, my poor baby boy is going to have a hard time understanding love, so please let my Flutter find a kind and understanding wife." She was worried that her son would choose the wrong woman, one who would take advantage of him and ultimately control him and every aspect in their married lives.

Flutter had an uneventful childhood with no recognitions of any kind in school. He was a below-average student whose grades were a far cry from his sister Janie's. Flutter, always by choice, sat in the back of the classroom slumped down in his chair so that his teachers would not see him or call him in the middle of a discussion. He wanted to blend into the background and not be noticed at all. Despite his lack of drive to excel in any subject in school, Flutter made it to the twelfth grade.

Now seventeen years old and another two inches taller, he was beginning to take on the appearance of a nice-looking young man. Some of the girls in his class began noticing him and giggled in the corners whenever he walked into the classroom. But Flutter was not interested in them as he thought they were fickle girls. He always took his chosen seat at the end of the last row in the last seat, and he would always go into his own world for the entire period in each class.

2

In November 1949, at the end of another uneventful school day, Flutter was preparing to walk the two miles home when something happened. He saw the most beautiful girl he had ever seen. He started to perspire profusely, but when he had the opportunity to speak to her, he was rendered speechless. This young woman had a beautiful smile, highlighted by two prominent dimples on either side of her face. He noticed that she had about the same complexion as he did (based on his mother's definition) and long, dark-brown hair that stopped an inch below her shoulders. She was about the height of his oldest sister, Elizabeth, who was about three inches shorter than him. Then Flutter noticed, of all things, her hourglass figure and shapely legs. Flutter thought, *Do all girls look like this? Why am I just now seeing this beautiful girl? Has she been at this school this whole time?*

Flutter noticed her walking down the hall, headed out of the school. He heard someone call her, and he now knew her name was Lily. When he got closer to her, she turned around, looked into his eyes, and smiled. All he could do then was walk past her and out the door. Flutter ran all the way home and went straight to his room. Unsure of what he was feeling, he sat on his bed just thinking about Lily.

During dinner, he was quieter than normal. It prompted his mother to ask, "Flutter, are you feeling all right?"

"Yes, ma'am," he replied dismissively.

After dinner, he sat on the porch and stared into the sky, not sure what he was going to do about this strange feeling fluttering in his chest. He was unable to sleep that night, but he was surprisingly not tired or sleepy the next day. His family was surprised that he was eager to leave the house after breakfast and get to school. He ran all the way there just as he had done the day before.

Upon entering the school, he found himself looking for Lily. As he got closer to his classroom, he saw her speaking to another classmate. He immediately stopped in his tracks and just stood there and stared at her for what seemed like an eternity. When the bell rang, all the students went into their respective classrooms. Much to his surprise, *she* walked into his classroom and sat in the first seat in the first row. He couldn't believe that this beautiful girl had been in his class the whole time and he had not noticed her.

Even though the seats were not assigned to the students, he felt compelled to sit in his self-assigned seat because he did not know what else to do. Not sure how any of it happened, he found himself listening to what was going on in the classroom; and to his surprise, he even knew the answer to one of the questions asked by his teacher, Mrs. Jackson. When no one raised their hands to answer this question, Flutter raised his.

His teacher asked, "Jeremy, is there something wrong?"

He replied, "No, Mrs. Jackson, I wanted to answer the question."

He saw his classmates turn around to look at him, the shock apparent on their faces. He even noticed Lily looking at him, smiling.

He was amazed at the words that came from his mouth but even more so when he was told that his answer was correct. His teacher acted as though he had said something profound. All of his classmates were astounded that he had actually participated in a class lesson, and just like that, they started seeing him in a different light.

Flutter noticed that Lily was still looking and smiling at him, and he felt his heart speed up. For the rest of that day, Flutter was happy about being in school. *Could this have anything to do with a certain dimpled-faced young woman?* He wasn't sure about that, but he suspected that it could be the case.

Even though Flutter was experiencing feelings he had never felt before, he was not sure what he was supposed to do or how he was supposed to act. Whenever there was an opportunity for one-on-one contact or conversation, Flutter would shy away or pretend as though he didn't see her.

Lily was totally confused by his actions, which she assumed were mere attempts to avoid her. Why he would want to do so, however, she had no idea. She tried on more than one occasion to speak to Flutter but always to no avail. She was beginning to think that maybe she had made a mistake at trying to get to know this perplexing young man.

3

For the next few weeks, nothing had visibly changed between Flutter and Lily. They still had not said anything to each other even though Lily had wanted to on more than a few occasions. She could not understand why Flutter would not speak to her. She was not aware that he had no idea how to hold a conversation with anyone let alone a beautiful young girl.

Flutter was having an equally difficult time trying to figure out what he was feeling and how to let Lily know that. Because he did not really have any friends at school, he had literally no one to speak to about what he was going through. What he did know was that he had feelings for a girl he hadn't—not even once—spoken to and did not even know how to begin a conversation with. He thought to himself more than once, *What should I do? Are these feelings normal?*

As spring approached, all the residents of their small town of approximately ten thousand residents were preparing for what needed to be done on their respective tracts of land. The normal chores of milking cows, slopping hogs, and feeding chickens were all commonplace rituals for each family.

Another ritual that the students were preparing for was the upcoming senior spring dance. This activity was a big deal for seniors because it marked the end of their years of schooling and the beginning of their adult lives. Many of them did not have plans to further their educations, but they had plans nonetheless: the boys all talked about enlisting, and the girls who were not planning to marry soon after graduation were going to nearby colleges, going to beauty school, or were helping out their families on their respective farms until marriage happened.

Then there was Flutter. He had not thought about what he would do after high school, but he had heard some of the boys talk about serving in the army. Unsure what that meant, he took the initiative to speak to Gene Mayfield, a boy in his class, about his plans after graduation. Gene told Flutter that he had already signed up to join the army and that he would be leaving town a month after graduation. Flutter heard all this intriguing information but was still uncertain as to what any of it meant. But he did start thinking that maybe this was something he wanted to do as well.

The students prepared for the upcoming dance: the girls made their party dresses, and the boys got their Sunday's-best suits ready. The graduating class of 1950 was a small class (of an even number) of forty-four students. There were more girls than boys, so the girls who had not already been asked by a boy had made plans to go together. No one thought this was odd. All the students were just excited about this event.

Not knowing what he was supposed to do, Flutter had not asked Lily to go to the dance with him. But, of course, because she was a very pretty girl, she had been asked by another boy. Unknown to him, she was hoping he would ask her to go with him; but deep down, she knew that wouldn't happen. She could not figure out why she had such strong feelings for a boy who had not even said hello to her.

However, Flutter did ask his mother to make sure his Sunday suit was ready for the dance. Octavia was beyond happy that her son was finally showing an interest in something, especially one as significant as the senior dance. She and her husband had noticed that in the last few months, Flutter's grades had improved, and they were still clueless as to what caused this. They had also been told by his teacher that he would indeed graduate, and they were happy that he had shown some interest in school this year. If only they knew it was all because of a girl.

4

The night of the spring dance, Flutter was nervous. Because both of his sisters were already married and living in their own homes close by, they each came by to see Flutter get ready and leave for his first dance. His sisters also tried to help out by telling him what to expect and what he was supposed to do.

Flutter could not imagine why there was so much fuss over a dance, but he had to admit that he was a little curious about what to expect.

"Have you asked a girl to go with you to the dance?" Janie asked him. He replied, "Why would I do that?" She tried to explain to her brother dating protocol, and she could tell that Flutter felt bad that he had not asked Lily to go with him. However, he thought maybe tonight would be his opportunity to say something to her for the first time.

His father let him drive the family truck to his first dance. It was then when he looked at his son differently, but he could not explain why. As Flutter drove off, his family stood on the porch waving to him as if he were moving away. As he got closer to the school, he heard the music and saw the lights in the school gym. The decorations had been done by some of his classmates. He finally saw what a decorated gym looked liked.

When he got up the nerve to walk into the noise-infested, brightly lit room, he was unable to move. He stood by the door and watched his classmates laugh, dance, eat, and have a good time. While standing there, he saw Lily and her date sitting at a table, immersed in conversation.

He slowly walked across the room; and to his amazement, his classmate and new friend, Gene, saw him and asked him to sit at his table. He too came alone, and Flutter took him up on his offer. "I have already danced with two girls," Gene commented. "And guess what, they asked me." Gene smiled.

"They asked you to dance?" Flutter asked him.

His sisters had not told him that, that was possible. They had tried to teach him a few steps though he was not entirely sure that he was even going to have an opportunity to use them. He refocused his attention on Lily and her date, and in the same moment that he did, she got up and walked out of the room.

Assuming she had gone to the ladies room, he thought this was his opportunity at last to have his first words with her. Flutter got up and quickly followed her, not really sure what words he was going to speak. As he waited for her to come out of the ladies room, he desperately tried to get his words together. The door opened, and several girls including Lily came out.

When Lily saw Flutter standing there, she decided that she was going to walk past him as he had done to her on many occasions before. However, this time, she heard him say, "Hi, Lily! I'm Flutter—I mean Jeremy Bernard Toliver, but my family calls me Flutter. I know that is a strange name, but my mother told me she gave me that name when I was born. She liked my long eyelashes or something like that."

"Hi, Jeremy." Lily smiled. "I already know who you are. I like the name Flutter. Do you mind if I call you Flutter?"

"No, you can call me Jeremy or Flutter," he responded with a smile on his face.

Flutter felt good about the conversation so far, and becoming more comfortable, he spoke further.

"Are you having a good time at the dance?"

"Yes, I am. What about you?"

"I guess I am too."

"Jeremy, why haven't you ever spoken to me? And why didn't you ask me to the dance tonight?"

Flutter did not expect these questions, so he had to think about his responses.

"I don't know. I guess I didn't know I was supposed to. I wanted to speak to you, but I couldn't."

Lily knew in that moment that Flutter was a sincere young man whom she really wanted to get to know. They stood in the hall and talked for another twenty minutes. He really learned a lot about Lily and began feeling some faint stirrings of something he had never felt before. The sweaty palms and heart palpitations had come back. Flutter was just then realizing that he only felt this way when he was around Lily. *Does this mean that I like her a lot?*

The boy who had taken Lily to the dance came looking for her, and when she saw him, she told Flutter that she would see him later. Not feeling like going back to the dance, he walked outside and decided to leave.

On his ride home, he thought about Lily and why he liked her so much. He also thought for the first time about what he would do after graduation and realized that he still had no idea. He thought about what his schoolmate Gene told him, and right then, he decided that he would go to the recruitment office the first chance he could and talk to them about joining the service.

He made a point of not telling his family about his plans, and for the first time in his life, he felt like he wanted to do something with it. He was sure this was because of Lily. He was really beginning to think about his future and what that future would look like with Lily in it.

5

Graduation day for the senior class of Parwell High School was very eventful. Parents were happy to see their sons and daughters walk across the gym stage and receive their diplomas. As the principal called Flutter's name (the real one), his entire family stood to their feet, applauded, and cheered loudly. They were so proud of him. After the rest of the class received their own diplomas, each family celebrated the day's events with a huge family meal in their respective homes.

Flutter and his family had a wonderful dinner that consisted of barbecue ribs and chicken, collard greens, corn on the cob, potato salad, and his mother's famous homemade rolls. For dessert, Octavia went all out and prepared her son's favorite desserts: there was banana pudding, blackberry cobbler, and homemade ice cream. Afterward, they all had festivities, which they enjoyed for the rest of the night.

While they all sat on the front porch talking about various subjects, Flutter took this opportunity to take the truck and drive over to Lily's house. Fortunately for him, no one noticed that he left. He had no intention of going inside her house; he just wanted to see if he could get a glimpse of her outside. The closer he got to her house, the more those feelings he had been experiencing in the last few weeks came back.

He parked the truck across from Lily's house, and to his surprise, he saw Lily sitting on a large rock by the creek in front of her house. She was just sitting alone, looking out across the creek. She was so preoccupied that she did not even notice Flutter coming up behind her.

Not knowing what to say to her, he merely tapped her shoulder. Surprised, she turned around quickly and said, "Flutter, you startled me!"

"I'm sorry. What are you doing here?"

"Believe it or not, I was thinking about you and what you were doing. I am really surprised you came to see me since you didn't say anything to me today during graduation."

With a deep breath, Flutter gave Lily an explanation that even surprised him.

"Lily, I am not sure what to say to you most of the time. I get these funny feelings every time I am around you, and my words don't seem to come. But I think I really like you, and I hope that's all right with you."

Lily smiled and grabbed his hand. "I was hoping you liked me because I like you too."

Of course, Flutter did not know what to do at this moment. He had no idea how to respond and instead blurted out, "I am going to the navy."

"You're going to the *navy*? When did you decide that?"

"About a month ago. I haven't told my parents yet."

"When do you plan on telling them, and why did you come over here tonight? Did you come here just to tell me you're leaving? Do you think I am going to *wait* for you, Jeremy Bernard Toliver?"

Not even waiting for a response, Lily got up and left Flutter sitting on the rock by himself. He waited for a few minutes, but Lily never came back. So he got back in his truck and drove home. He was so confused at what had just happened. He asked himself so many questions, but he had no answers to any of them. When he got back home, he went straight to his room and stared at the ceiling the rest of the night.

Octavia saw this change in her son but still couldn't put her finger on the cause. She noticed that he asked to borrow the truck more now than she could ever remember, and to her amazement, whenever he did, he would go and visit Gene. Gene even came to visit Flutter on several occasions. His mother was glad that her son had a friend, but she still found it a little unsettling as this was so unlike him. She also found that he had changed so much physically. To her he even looked older—more like a young man. She decided that she was going to have a talk with him when he returned.

6

During his visit with Gene, they both talked about going into the service and what that actually meant. He also talked to Gene about his last conversation with Lily.

"Gene, I really like Lily, and she said she likes me too. Can you believe that?" Flutter confessed.

"Did you kiss her yet?" Gene asked him.

"No, why do you ask me that?"

"Because when you like girls, you're supposed to kiss them."

This was all new information to Flutter, and he and Gene ended up talking for the rest of the morning about man things.

While Flutter was having these intense conversations with his friend Gene about girls and the world, back home, his mother was accepting a certified letter for him. She and her husband were curious as to why their son would be receiving this kind of mail from the government, but after a few moments' thought, they assumed it was news about registering for the draft. Still, all they could talk about was what was going on with their son lately and the mail he just received.

In the middle of their conversation, Flutter walked in. The moment he did, however, he immediately saw his parents' expressions of confusion. His mother spoke first.

"Flutter you got some mail today. Your father thinks this may be a draft notification."

After a few moments of hesitation, he took the letter from his mother, slowly opened it, glanced over it, and handed it to his mother. Octavia took all of two minutes to read the letter and then looked at her son with an astonished and puzzled look on her face. She handed the letter to her husband, who did not appear as astonished as she did.

"Son, why did we have to find out this way? Why couldn't you have told us your plans or at least discussed them with us before you enlisted?"

These questions were how Jacob started the inquisition on his son, leading to a long conversation between the three of them.

"Father, I was going to tell you and Mama today. I didn't know this would come in the mail so soon…My friend told me he had signed up and he was leaving after graduation. So I went down and spoke to the navy recruiter before graduation, and he told me I couldn't join until I was eighteen. So two weeks after graduation, Gene went with me. And I signed up.

He's going to the army, but I want to go to the navy. The sergeant at the recruiting office told me that if I joined right out of high school, he would cut my enlistment to four and a half years instead of six. I know I didn't talk to you all about this, but if I am old enough to join the navy, I think that I am old enough to make my own decisions."

While Jacob and Octavia were upset at the thought of their son volunteering to serve in the military, they were proud of him for taking some initiative and interest in something. Right then, the only words either of them thought and finally spoken by his mother were, "When do you leave?"

"In two weeks."

At that, Octavia started to cry and hugged her baby boy. And even though Jacob could not verbalize it, he was proud of his son. He thought, *That's my son.* For the first time in a very long time, Flutter and his parents had a long talk—long enough that it lasted well into the wee hours of the morning. Each one left this long conversation thinking and wishing they'd had this time before now.

For the next two weeks, the Toliver family spent practically every waking moment together and valued the time they had left.

The day before he was supposed to report, he decided to go and say good-bye to Lily. When he arrived in front of her house, those same fluttery feelings he had experienced whenever he was close to her returned. Twenty minutes passed before he got up the nerve to knock on the door. As he was trying to gather his words, the door opened. Lily just stood there without speaking, staring at him.

Just as Flutter was going to say hello, Lily exclaimed, "What do you want, Jeremy?"

Surprised at Lily's tone when she spoke his given name and too shy to know how to respond, he replied, "I'm leaving for the navy tomorrow, and I came over to tell you good-bye."

"Good-bye. I cannot believe you had the nerve to come and see me the day before you leave! Do you even care about me, Jeremy Toliver?"

"Why did you ask me that question?"

"Never mind. Forget I asked. Good-bye. And have a good life in the navy!"

With that, Lily slammed the door, ran to her room, and burst into tears. Flutter stood on her porch speechless and uncertain what had just happened. As he turned to walk away, he suddenly got his nerve up and knocked on her door for a second time. When Lily opened the door, he saw that she had been crying.

"Lily, I couldn't leave until we cleared things up. I know I didn't—don't—always say the right things or ask you to go places or come to see you regularly, but I really do like you. A lot. I guess I just came by to let you know that."

He was surprised at himself for even being able to get the words out.

Surprised at the newly talkative Flutter, Lily replied, "Why did you wait to tell me this when you are about to leave town for a long time? I always wondered if I had done something to upset you or if you just didn't like me because you never seemed interested in getting to know me. I liked you the first time I saw you in the seventh grade, but you never noticed me. So what do we do now that you're leaving?"

Flutter could not believe that he had not noticed Lily before their last year in high school but even more so that *she* had noticed *him*. Now with more confidence, he replied, "We do nothing until I get back."

That was all Flutter said, and just when he was turning to walk away, Lily caught his arm, spun him around, and gently kissed him on the lips. He suddenly felt a warm, flushed feeling all over his body. This was a new feeling for Flutter. As usual, not knowing what to say, he cupped her face with both of his hands, said good-bye, and walked away.

Many questions went through Lily's head, and she just stood there as she had no answers to any of them. But at that moment, Lily saw her future, and she knew she wanted to be Mrs. Jeremy Toliver. Her tears of despair suddenly turned into tears of happiness for the man whom she knew, at this moment, she dearly loved.

7

In the almost four years since Flutter left Parwell, life in the Toliver family had changed quite a bit. Octavia had assumed the running of the household since her husband, Jacob, had suffered a severe stroke. The doctor told her that he had to cut back on his daily chores due to his paralysis on the left side of his body. Given these new circumstances, Octavia sold much of their livestock and even some of their land (about fifty acres) to help with her husband's medical bills.

Their two oldest children, Beth and Janie, had become parents of one and two children, respectively. Both young women had made sure that with whatever help that their parents needed, they and their husbands were available to assist them each and every day.

And then there was Flutter.

He was not good at writing letters or calling his family (any type of communication, really). In the last four years, he had written one letter per year, and all four letters basically said the same thing. From his letters, his family couldn't be sure when their son was coming home. He never told his parents how to write to him, so basic communication was nonexistent. Because of this, Flutter never knew that his father had been ill. Not only had there been no communication with his family, there had also been no communication with Lily while he was gone. In his mind, she was waiting on him to return and to start their lives together. While his absence made his heart grow fonder for Lily, his absence only frustrated Lily more. So much so that her thoughts and attention had allowed herself to entertain the company and conversation of another young man. Lily's thoughts were always on Flutter, but her thoughts were now being divided between a life with Flutter or a life with another.

Though she was not a regular churchgoer anymore since her husband's stroke, Octavia still attended Wednesday night prayer service meetings at their small community church, New Hope Baptist Church. Her nightly prayers always included a request that the Lord watch over her son and bring him back home safely. She also requested that the Lord strengthen her and take away her fears of losing her husband and her son. After these prayers, she made a point of reading various scriptures from the books of Psalms and Proverbs. She also read these same scriptures to Jacob, and every night for the past year, he occasionally asked her to read the first two verses of Psalm 18 (KJV) to him. As she read, he repeated the verses aloud.

"'I will love thee, O LORD, my strength. The LORD is my rock, and my fortress, and my deliverer; my God, my strength, in whom I will trust; my buckler, and the horn of my salvation, my high tower.'"

Every time, Jacob ended by saying, "Thank you, Lord." Before going to sleep, Jacob and Octavia always talked about their family and what they had been through in the last four years. They felt blessed by the Lord and knew that he would take care of their son and continue protecting their family. They would then fall asleep with calm hearts from the knowledge that the Lord was in control of their lives.

Lily had not heard from Flutter since he left for the navy. She knew she loved him, but her anger and frustration at his seeming lack of interest in her made her rethink her earlier thoughts of waiting for him and then marrying him.

Life for Lily and her family had gone through some changes as well. Her father had died in a tractor accident six months after Flutter left for the navy. She did not even know how to contact him to let him know of this news. Also, within this time that Flutter had been away, Lily had indeed become very serious about a young man whom she had gotten to know and was very interested in a more-than-friends relationship with her.

She had been honest with him and told him about Flutter and her feelings for him. He did not pressure her but made sure that she knew he was there if and when she changed her mind. She had to admit that she did not feel for him as she did for Flutter but contrary to popular belief, separation does not always make the heart grow fonder.

Flutter was going to have a lot to digest when he returned home.

8

The day started just like any other in the small town of Parwell, Texas. It was windy with overcast clouds that hid the sun most of the day; there were no signs of rain. The residents were up early and, by 11:00 a.m., had already done a full day of chores.

Octavia had not slept well the night before, but she did not know why. She had an unusual feeling when she got up that morning, but she started her day just as she normally did. Jacob did one chore, which was to feed the small number of chickens they still had, while Octavia washed and hung the clothes to dry.

Beth's husband, Timothy, had come by to bring supplies from the hardware store in town. Since Jacob was not able to do many of the chores that had to be completed in a day, his two sons-in-law had divvied up the things to be done between themselves, and it was working fine.

As Octavia went into the house to prepare lunch, she suddenly became very nervous and dropped a platter of meat she was about to put on the table. Before she could begin cleaning up the mess, there was a knock on the door. Her heart started to race, and she had a sinking feeling in her stomach. As she was slowly walking to the door, her thoughts went to Flutter.

She slowly entered the room from the kitchen while Jacob arrived in the room from the bedroom, and they met at the door at the same time. They looked at each other, thinking the same thing. Jacob took his wife's hand, and he slowly opened the door. When the door opened, there stood a man dressed in a military uniform and holding a letter.

"Mr. and Mrs. Toliver, my name is Sergeant Riley. I'm from the navy, and I would like to speak to you about your son, Jeremy Bernard Toliver."

Tears quickly pooled in Octavia's eyes as she began thinking the worst.

"Yes, please come in," Jacob replied.

"What has happened to our son?" Octavia asked.

"Mrs. Toliver, I believe all of your questions will be answered after you read this letter."

As they both read the words on the paper, Octavia's tears changed from ones of dread to ones of thankfulness. The letter said,

> Mr. and Mrs. Toliver,
>
> Seaman Jeremy Bernard Toliver has been wounded in a combat exercise, and he is currently in the military hospital in Norfolk, Virginia. As this injury is not life threatening, it is, however, to the extent that Seaman Toliver cannot complete his current enlistment in its entirety. He is being honorably discharged before his tour of duty is over. He will remain in the hospital for two more weeks, and only then will he receive a military escort home. The navy is grateful to have had a man of your son's caliber to serve our country.
>
> Sincerely,
> Captain Lee Andrews
> USS *Orion*

Tears flowed freely from both Jacob's and Octavia's eyes. They were both proud of their son, but more than that, they were relieved and happy that he would be coming home soon. They took this time to contact Beth and Janie to let them know the good news and to plan a homecoming for their military son.

In the next Wednesday night prayer service, Octavia told the congregation about her son and that he would be coming home. She invited her church family to be a part of their homecoming celebration.

The day ended for Octavia and Jacob with thanks to the Lord for having answered their prayers and sending their son home. They couldn't wait to see Flutter, who had turned into a man without any help from them.

9

It was a sunny day in August 1954. For two days, Octavia had been cooking and preparing all of her son's favorite meals, and some of her neighbors had volunteered to bring various dishes as well. People usually didn't bring food to a neighbor's house unless there was a funeral or a house wedding reception, but this was a happy occasion (and the food was welcomed).

The Tolivers did not know exactly when Flutter would arrive. They had been up since the break of day making sure that the house was cleaned, the food was cooked, and the Welcome Home signs were hung and visible from corner to corner.

At around 2:00 p.m., a plain dark-colored car turned onto the Tolivers' street and slowly pulled in front of the decorated house. All the family members, neighbors, and church attendees were on the porch waiting to see and hug their relative and friend. The passenger's side door opened, and out came Seaman Toliver dressed in his navy uniform. He positioned his crutches to walk, consequently displaying his leg injury.

Not able to wait any longer, his parents and sisters ran to him, hugged him, and kissed him. They had smiles on their faces and happy tears in their eyes. Jacob hugged his son and gave him a hard handshake—his way to let him know how proud of him he was. Flutter was all smiles as well and was happy to see his family, whom he had not seen in about four years.

After about fifteen minutes of greetings and meetings, everyone went inside to continue the celebration with food. After several hours of celebrating, some of the neighbors and other invited guests started leaving. They all expressed their happiness at meeting Flutter and wished him a speedy recovery.

After everyone had gone home, Flutter took this opportunity to explain to his family what he had experienced in the last few years and what had happened to him when he got his injury. It seemed that Flutter's assignment while in the navy was repairing combat planes, and if asked, he had to admit that he was actually quite good at it.

His family acknowledged how grown-up Flutter had become, how his appearance had changed from a shy and thin boy into a muscular self-confident man. Before going to bed for the night, Flutter told his parents that he was glad to be home and that he wanted to help out as much as possible when his leg healed a little more. He was then told about his father's stroke and the limited amount of farm chores he could do since his illness, and as evidence of his maturity, he wasted no time in telling his parents how he intended to assist them in every way he could.

His last words to them on his first day home were that he wanted to speak to them about something important in the morning. They were not sure what to expect but figured that they would get answers in the morning. Before long, they all bid one another good night and kissed each other a last time before they went to bed.

10

The next morning, another happy family mealtime was arranged. There was a huge breakfast prepared for the son who had arrived from his military exploits. Unsure when he would awaken, Jacob and Octavia made sure to move around carefully so as not to disturb him. Finally, around midmorning, Flutter came into the room ready for his mother's homemade biscuits.

Even though he had already spent the entirety of the previous day visiting with his parents, they still found plenty to talk about. Flutter told them about what he had learned while in the navy, the places he had seen and been to, and the friends he had made. His parents both looked at each other in astonishment during this conversation. Without speaking a word to each other, they both knew that this young man was not the same young man who left them four years ago.

After breakfast, Flutter told his parents that he wanted to speak with them about something. They all went out onto the back porch and into the cool fresh air and seated themselves amongst Octavia's daisies. Flutter started the conversation, telling them about what his plans were for the future. Being in the military had taught him a lot about repairing equipment and vehicles; and this training helped him secure a job repairing airplanes in the maintenance department at an airport in Dallas, Texas.

He explained his new job responsibilities to his parents who were extremely proud of their son and very surprised at the changes they were noticing with every word that came from his mouth. He went on to explain when he would be leaving to move to Dallas as well as the rest of his plans. The next part of Flutter's conversation with his parents was about something that he had never discussed with them before. He was not sure how to begin, so he just blurted out the words.

"I know I have never said a word about Lily, but I met her in high school and…I love her. I have thought about her the entire time I was away, and after I was sure I got the job at the airport, I knew the next step was to ask her to marry me."

Uncertain how to respond or if they actually heard him correctly, his parents looked at each other with probably the same train of thought. Then his mother spoke the only words she could muster and dare to speak.

"Flutter, this is news to us. This is the first time you have ever said anything to us about a woman. Are you sure? When do we get to meet her? Does she feel the same way you do?"

"I know you have questions, but just please let me say this. Yes, I am very sure about loving Lily, and I do not know when we will get married. But I am pretty sure she feels the same way about me, and I was thinking I could bring her over to meet the family this weekend. I start my new job in six months, so I would like to spend this time finding a place to live in Dallas and then asking her to marry me. I would like a small ceremony, but I will need to speak to her about that first. If it's okay, I will bring her here for dinner Saturday so that she can meet everyone."

"Saturday…That is two days away. What does she like to eat so that I know what to cook?"

"I do not know, but I am sure whatever you fix will be great."

Jacob had been quiet during this whole discourse between Mother and Son, but now he had to say something.

"Flutter, why is there such a rush to get married? Have you thought about the responsibilities that a man has when he takes a wife? Have you considered that she may say no? Have you even spoken to her about marriage? I just do not want you disappointed if things do not go the way you want them to. Your mother and I are concerned for you."

"I appreciate your concern, Father, but I have thought this through. No, I do not know that she will say yes, but I know she feels the same way about me as I do about her. I plan on going to see her later today and discussing with her the future. Our future."

Perplexed and confused, his parents, in turn, said that they were happy for him if this is what he wanted and that they would be happy to meet Lily on Saturday. After further conversation about Flutter's time in the service and his future plans, they just hugged him and wished him well.

As Octavia hugged her son, tears of happiness, sadness, and confusion at his future flowed down her cheeks. This new Jeremy was indeed the man they always knew he was capable of becoming. Despite her happiness from getting to know this new Flutter, she felt a dread that she could not explain. *How do I explain these feelings to him?* The words would not come, so she hugged him for as long as she could.

11

Later that day, Flutter decided to go and see Lily after not having seen her for four years. He had not written to her or communicated with her in any manner. This fact did not seem to matter to him because in his mind, she loved him as he loved her, and nothing—not even time—could change that.

Before he went to see Lily, he drove to see his two sisters and their families and told them about his plans, and like their parents, they were amazed at what he was saying. They were happy for their brother and told him so, but none of them wanted to tell him about the certainty that he was going to get his heart broken. After spending the rest of the morning and part of the afternoon with his family, he bid his sisters good-bye, got into the car, and left for Lily's house.

He enjoyed this drive to his future wife's house and took his time, taking in the scenery of his hometown. He discovered that not much had changed since he had been gone.

When he arrived at his destination, he slowly walked to the door and knocked softly. His movements were in no way hurried because in his mind, everything was the same as it was during the last conversation he had with Lily all those years ago. He expected that when Lily would see him, she would hug him tightly and kiss him passionately. (Not that he knew what passionately actually meant or felt or looked like, but he was preparing for it anyway.)

Lily's mother opened the door. Flutter did not expect anyone but Lily to answer the door, so he was caught off guard. He explained that he was there to see Lily. Her mother said that she was at the church for rehearsal. She gave him directions and told him that she was on her way there as well. He then thanked her and said goodbye. He told himself, *That would be my new mother-in-law. She seems like a nice woman.*

He found the church easily with the directions he had been given. He noticed that there were not many cars at the church, so he found a close parking spot and proceeded to go inside. Flutter had decided that he would sit in the back of the church and wait for Lily to finish her choir rehearsal.

As he walked into the church, he saw about seven people standing near the altar. He tried to figure out what type of choir rehearsal this was. The main door opened, and he spotted Lily's mother walking inside, making her way to the front of the church. Suddenly he heard a voice say, "The mother of the bride will be sitting here on this pew."

Mother of the bride? Lily's mother is the mother of the bride? Does Lily have another sister getting married? In that moment, he saw Lily turn around and smile at her mother. Flutter's heart started pounding, but this time, it was a different type of pounding from what he had previously experienced when he was around Lily.

Flutter was now seeing that this rehearsal was a *wedding* rehearsal. For Lily. He noticed the man standing next to her. He stood about six foot four and weighed about 210 pounds. He had a mustache and was wearing what looked to be a three-piece suit. He also had a large smile on his face. He had never seen this man before, so he was sure that he was not from Parwell. *How long has she known this man? Why is she marrying him? And why didn't she wait for me to return?* These were all questions he intended to ask Lily.

12

When the rehearsal came to an end, Flutter saw Lily kiss the stranger. Flutter's stomach dropped. But that wasn't all. He also noticed how happy she looked—he could practically see her dimples from where he was sitting!

Shortly thereafter, people who were in the rehearsal were walking out of the church, and Lily was one of the last ones to walk his way. The closer she got to him, the more she recognized him. When she was absolutely certain that it was him, her smile went away. She stood there without speaking and told her fiancé that she would meet him outside.

No one spoke right away; they both just stared at each other.

Finally, Flutter spoke, frustration lacing his tone, "What are you doing here? I thought you were going to wait for me to return? How long have you known this guy? Had you already made plans to marry him before I left?"

Lily took her time to respond because she wanted to choose her words carefully.

"First of all, Mr. Toliver, since I did not hear from you in *four* years, I assumed you were no longer interested in us. Second, I met James two years after you left, and I got to know him. Unlike you, he told me he loved me each and every day, and there was no question in my mind what his intentions were.

He asked me to marry him a year ago, and believe it or not, I thought about *you*. But since I did not know how to contact you because you did not write to me, it was clear to me you no longer cared—*if* you ever cared—so I said yes…The wedding will be on

Saturday, and believe it or not, I am happy without you. I do not understand you and have never understood you. I do not even know why I thought I was in love with you in the first place."

Flutter stared at Lily and had a different kind of feeling in his stomach. He felt like he was going to be sick and about to throw up but couldn't. He did not know what to say, but what finally came out of his mouth surprised even him.

"Lily, I love you. I am sorry I did not write to you, but I didn't think you were expecting me to. I just thought we would get married and move to Dallas. I already have a job there at the airport. Everything was worked out in my head, and I wanted to surprise you today."

"Flutter, why did it take you this long to tell me all this? Do you know how long I have waited for you to tell me even a fraction of what you just said? I knew the first time I saw you that you were the one for me. But you never told me that you felt the same way. I was just *hoping* that you felt the same way and that we would start a life together."

Lily began crying. Flutter now knew that everything she said was what he'd wanted to say to her but never was able to.

"Lily, I am so sorry. I have never been good with words or knowing what to say or do in certain circumstances. I too *did* know the first time I saw you. You were the one for me. I dreamt about you almost every night when I was away, and my dreams always ended with us getting married. *Please* forgive me. You can't go through with this wedding now. We love each other, and it should be *us* getting married!"

Lily cried uncontrollably now, her sobs rendering her speechless. When she regained her composure, she said, "Flutter, I love you. With all my heart. But I do love James as well. As much as I love you and want to be with you, I am going through with my wedding on Saturday. I have never met your family, and you have not met mine. Why is that? Did you even know that my father died six months after you left? It was like I never existed in your life. I may have once imagined my life with you, but now that life will be with James."

With that, Lily kissed him gently on the cheek, walked away, and left Flutter standing there. He did not follow her or even try to stop her from leaving. He knew that everything she said was the truth, and he could not deny it.

Instead of leaving the church and going home, Flutter sat in the corner of the last pew, in the dark much in the same way he sat in class many years ago. Not wanting to be noticed.

The Saturday he had planned on his family meeting his future bride was now going to be the day she was marrying another man. *How can I explain this to my family? How can I explain this to myself?*

13

Flutter explained to his family that there was no longer going to be a wedding. Each and every day since then, they saw his pain and anguish, so they did not ask him any questions. Over the next six months, Flutter's leg healed to the point where he only had a small limp that was not that noticeable. He busied himself with helping out his parents around the house and in the fields. He did everything he could to keep himself busy to hopefully distract himself from the pain that did not let up.

But this did not work. He kept thinking about Lily and the mistakes he had made with her. He never knew that loving someone as he did Lily could hurt so much. When he went to town, he saw Lily on her occasional visits to Parwell to see her mother, but he always made sure that she did not see him. The pain felt as though it would never go away, so he was looking forward to his move to Dallas in a few days.

Flutter's family again felt the need to give him a going-away get-together. Knowing that they were going to do it, he insisted on keeping it to just family. Octavia made the meal Flutter requested and kept it a low-key gathering.

No one asked any questions about marriage plans. No one even brought up Lily's name. But they all saw the pain and hurt in his eyes and in his every movement. Octavia and Jacob hated to see their son experiencing the pain from losing one's first love, but there was nothing they could do to help him.

That same night, no one in the Toliver household could sleep for various reasons, so it was no wonder that the night seemed to drag on forever.

After breakfast the next morning, Flutter got ready to leave. There were no long good-byes. He had already put all his belongings into a secondhand truck he had purchased after he returned home, so all he had to do was get into his truck and leave his hometown for the second time. He had initially thought that he would not be taking this trip alone but with a wife, but that just wasn't to be.

On his trip out of town, he made a point of driving by Lily's mother's house hoping that he would see a glimpse of the woman who had taken his heart but not his last name. He knew she did not live in that house anymore, but he still got those same quivering feelings that he had become so used to when he was around wherever Lily was or had been. He did not see his Lily, however, but that did not stop those feelings.

Jeremy Bernard Toliver was about to embark on a new chapter in his life *alone*, but he was determined to go on. Deep down, though it hurt him, he wished Lily and her new husband a happy future.

14

Flutter quickly settled into his new home and job mainly because he had nothing but his thoughts to occupy himself with. However, many of his thoughts still featured Lily. He could not believe how his life had taken such a different turn. It didn't seem like it's already been two and a half years since he arrived in Dallas alone.

Never quite able to be more social, Flutter had only made one friend: Charles Duffy. He was someone he met at work. Outside of work in their spare time, they often went to sporting events; and on several occasions, Charles even invited Flutter to his home to have dinner with his wife and children.

"My wife's cooking some of her famous fried catfish tonight. I told her I was going to invite you, so she is cooking enough for an army," Charles would say to entice his friend.

He felt comfortable with Charles, and for now, that was enough; he never thought of meeting a woman to settle down with and having a family of his own (not since Lily, at least). Even though he had made no plans of finding a wife, it seemed that fate was going to step in for him.

On a warm summer day in July 1957, Flutter decided to go to the grocery store to purchase some items. Unknown to him, his life was going to change in that moment—whether it was for better or for worse was yet to be determined.

While paying for his recent purchases at the checkout counter, a woman in the next line noticed him and made a point of getting his attention. She spoke to him as he was walking away. He turned to look at the woman, who had also managed to get everyone else's attention in the neighboring checkout lines with her loud remarks.

"I bet your wife loves you for buying the groceries."

Unsure if she was actually speaking to him, Flutter did not respond. He just looked at her.

"I wish I had a man who would do that for me."

Again, Flutter did not respond.

As she finished paying for her own groceries, she walked over to Flutter, looked inside his grocery bags, and then said, "I see you only have enough for one person…Aren't you married?"

Surprised at how forward this woman was and with what she was asking him, he said, "I have to go."

Not taking that as a proper reply, the woman followed him to his truck.

"My name is Joyceanne Gafford, but you can call me Anne." He did not offer any information about himself. "And if I'm not being too forward, what is your name?"

"My name is Jeremy," Flutter reluctantly responded. No other information was offered. Anne seemed satisfied with only knowing his first name. And if that wasn't strange enough, she gave him a small card, which included her telephone number and home address. He glanced at the information, not at all interested.

Excusing himself quickly, he left Anne standing in the parking lot. Not really paying attention to her as he left, Flutter drove away without noticing that this strange woman was following him in her car. He did not live very far from the store, so in approximately ten minutes, he was pulling into his driveway. Still unaware of what was happening, he was getting out of his truck when he saw Anne's car driving forward. She did not stop her car.

Anne had accomplished her mission: to find out where he lived.

He stood outside for a few minutes looking at her car as she drove off into the distance. He tried to figure out why she followed him and what all this meant. He was so naïve, merely shrugging it off with the thought, *Maybe Anne lives somewhere close to my home, and this is the way she took to get there.*

15

Over the next six months, Anne just happened to "run into" Flutter at least ten times: whether it was at the grocery store, in front of his house, around the corner at church, or even at his job, Anne was definitely trying to insinuate herself into Flutter's life. Even though he had not provided her with any information but his first name, Anne knew not only where he shopped and where he lived but also where he went to church and where he worked. Because he was so trusting and not familiar with feminine wiles, he had no idea what was really happening.

Because Anne had planned them all to happen, they had actually had several conversations during their "chance encounters." Flutter had to admit that Anne was an attractive woman (though not as attractive as Lily). She stood approximately five foot five and weighed about 135 pounds. She had a nice smile, but Flutter noticed that many of her facial features were always accented with various eye shadow colors, red cheeks, and red lips. Her hair was shoulder length and was of an auburn color that he had never seen before, but he thought that it looked good against her dark-brown skin color.

Flutter learned that Anne had a three-year-old son from a previous relationship (although it was not a marriage). He also found her to be a very independent woman. She worked as a nurse's aide at Pinkston Clinic and lived not far from it in a part of the city known as Arlington Heights. She had one brother who lived somewhere in Oklahoma, and his name was Byron Jennings. Flutter wondered but never asked why they had different last names given the fact that Anne had never been married.

Flutter and Anne's encounters have become so frequent that it was no longer unusual for him to see her at least three times in a week. He had grown accustomed to her bringing him lunch on his job or suggesting that they do things together like picnics or dinners. Flutter's friend, Charles, would often smile and say, "You don't know it, Jeremy, but she wants you. You better be careful if you're not planning on marrying her."

He didn't know what to make of this comment as marriage had not even entered his mind since Lily. He never imagined spending his life with anyone but Lily, so talking or thinking about marriage with Anne never occurred to him.

All this talk about marriage had made Flutter homesick. He had not seen his family in over two years, so he decided to take a trip home. He told no one of his impending trip except his friend, Charles. "I just need to see my family," he said. So on a sunny and cold winter day, he took the hour-and-a-half trip to Parwell, Texas.

The closer he got to his hometown, the more his thoughts went to the last time he saw Lily and the conversation they had then. While he couldn't wait to see his family, Flutter was hoping to catch a glimpse of Lily. He wasn't sure if she lived in Parwell, but he was definitely going to find out. While he had not forgotten Lily was a married woman, he chose to just focus on everything about Lily, except for the reason they couldn't be together.

16

On his first trip home since he started life on his own, Jeremy Bernard "Flutter" Toliver was coming home. He drove around slowly, taking in the sights as a tourist would do if they were in a never before seen place. He saw Mr. Harrison's Feed and Tackle still in business. Around the corner, Mrs. Wilson's Sewing Emporium was still booming with the ladies from the church crochet club in attendance. And Murford's Car Garage and Gas Station still had cars waiting to be checked out by the owner, Murt. Nothing had changed that Flutter could tell; the small town was as he had left it.

Before going to see his family, he decided to drive by Lily's family home just on the off chance he might see her visiting her mother. As he pulled over in front of the house, he began sweating as he had done so many times before. He was sitting in the car when the front door of her home opened and he noticed a familiar sight. It was Lily opening the door and coming out to hang some rugs on the clothesline to dry. She had not changed at all; she was still that beautiful young girl who captured his heart in high school all those years ago.

Flutter thought, *Maybe her marriage had not lasted, and she's single and waiting for me.* He knew that these were terrible thoughts to have, but he couldn't help thinking that maybe the Lord had heard his silent prayers for him and Lily to get to have a life together. He decided to take a chance and approach her. As he slowly got out of his truck, she noticed him and stopped what she was doing to meet him halfway.

"Hi, Lily" was all he could say.

"Hello, Jeremy. How are you?"

Oh, how formal she is being, Flutter thought. "I am fine. What about you?"

"I can't complain…It's been a while. I heard you moved to Dallas and have a job there."

"Yes, I have been there a little over two years. What about you? Are you still living in Parwell?"

"Yes, my mother died a few months after my wedding. It was sudden, and since she left me the house, my husband and I decided to move here for now. He travels a lot, so this move was not a problem for him…I finally met your mother at my mother's funeral. It seemed that my mother had met Mrs. Toliver at one of the Wednesday night prayer meetings and they became good friends.

I didn't realize she was your mother until she came to the house after the funeral and introduced herself to me. She told me she had a son named Jeremy, whom she called Flutter and went to high school and was about my age, so we figured out it must be you. It's a small world, isn't it? Your sister Beth came with her, and she brought me a beautiful plant. I really appreciated that. We have stayed in contact, and we try to get together about once a week."

The only words Flutter heard during this long explanation about her mother's death and funeral were *my husband.* His heart had literally stopped beating because she had answered the only question he needed answered. She was indeed still married and was apparently living in Parwell, Texas. And to add to his confusion, Lily now knew his mother and had become friends with his sister Beth.

"You know, Flutter, I shouldn't even be telling you this, but I still think about you every day. I love my husband—and we are even talking about having a baby—but I do wish I was having that conversation with you instead. You do not know how much I loved and *still* love you, Flutter. I know I should not be saying any of this now, but I want you to know what we could have had if only you had written to me once. That would have changed our future—our present—drastically. We would have been together forever…Just know that my love for you will never fade away."

"Lily, I will never forgive myself for not having known how to tell you what you meant to me. I just thought that you would wait for me no matter what. It is my fault that we cannot be together now. But like you said, my love for you will always be there…I must go now before I am unable to leave. I am glad you finally met my mother and my sister Beth. You know, she would have loved having another daughter and sounds like you and Beth have become sisters."

With those last words, Flutter left Lily standing in her yard. The last thing of her that he caught sight of was her hair blowing in the wind. *That should have been my wife*, he thought. However, somehow, he knew that this wasn't going to be the last time he saw Lily; he was going to make sure of that. On the way to his parents', all he could think of was Lily and how his life could be different with her in it.

Flutter had a good visit and a long conversation with his family. He explained to his parents how he felt about Lily and how his inability to tell her had cost them both a life together. His mother was very understanding.

"Flutter, I have gotten to know Lily, and I see why you love her. She is a lovely young woman, and I have gotten to know her and love her like a daughter. Beth feels the same way about her." His father could see how this young woman had affected his son, but he did not have the words to console him.

"Everything will work out for you, Flutter," she told him. "The Lord will send you a nice woman. I believe that."

He took those words with him and said good-bye to his family until the next visit (whenever that would be).

17

The last conversation Flutter had with Lily stayed in his mind day in and day out: he thought about her when he went to bed at night and when he opened his eyes in the morning. He was still convinced that he and Lily would be together someday.

On his first day back at work since his trip home, he heard Charles say, "You have changed, Jeremy. What happened to you when you went home?" He knew that Charles was right; he had changed, but he could not explain how or why he had changed. Perhaps it was because his life was empty. And that, he knew why.

Thinking about what his mother told him about the Lord sending him a nice woman, he wondered if he had already met her. *Is Anne the woman Mama talked about? Do I want a ready-made family the moment I say, "I do"? Could I ever feel the same way about Anne as I do about Lily?*

His maternal grandmother, Birdie, always told him, "If a woman won't go to church with you, then you don't want to spend the rest of your life with her." He made a decision at this moment to ask Anne to go to church with him this coming Sunday. He thought he knew what his grandmother meant by this statement.

He did have Anne's telephone number, but he had never called it, so he wasn't sure where he put the card with her contact information. He decided that he would just have to wait until she "ran into him" again (which would probably be today or tomorrow). Flutter told Charles what he planned to do, and in turn, his friend told him how he felt about this decision.

"Jeremy, I get a funny feeling about this woman Anne. She seems so pushy and controlling. If she is this way now—and you don't even know her that well—think about how she would act if you showed any interest in her. Also, remember she has a son, and where there is a child, there is also a parent somewhere. I talked to my wife about this and how forward I thought she was, and she told me to tell you to be careful."

"Be careful. Careful about what? To be honest with you, I never even gave Anne a second thought, so I never really thought about dating her anyway. Maybe she is just trying to tell me she is interested in me and wants me to be interested in her."

Unsure what to say at this point, Charles repeated his warning one last time, "Just be careful and move slowly. *Very* slow."

As Flutter had predicted, Anne stopped by his job later that day "to say hello" (was her excuse). He took this opportunity to ask her to go to church with him Sunday, and before he even finished talking, Anne answered in the affirmative. She was all smiles and quickly told him that she would be at his house thirty minutes before the service began because she hated to be late for anything. Flutter was surprised at how this immediately felt like this was Anne's idea, at how she had taken over the plans.

"My son and I will see you bright and early Sunday morning, so be ready," she said as she left him standing in the doorway with a puzzled look on his face. She did agree to go to church with him, so he thought that this would make his grandmother happy. *But what about my happiness?*

As promised, come Sunday morning, Anne and her son, Richard, were at his house promptly at 10:00 a.m. Flutter noticed she was nicely dressed, but what caught his eye was that she had on more makeup than usual. Her son seemed polite, and when Flutter asked him how he was doing, he responded, "I am fine, sir."

After some small talk and a few minutes of enduring Anne's comments about his house needing a woman's touch, they left for church. At the end of the service, they both agreed that it was inspirational and that they should attend more often. Flutter was prepared to say his good-byes to Anne and her son, but she had other plans: she told him that she was cooking dinner at his house. Then she promptly gave him a grocery list of items she needed to prepare her signature fried-chicken dinner.

"Take Richard with you while I stay at home and straighten up a bit. Hurry back though 'cause I'm starving," she demanded. Not wanting to cause trouble, Flutter did what he was asked to do, and he and little Richard drove off to the store.

When they arrived back home and upon entering the house, Flutter noticed that Anne had taken the liberty of moving some furniture around in every room of the small house. He was speechless but quickly responded to the new changes when Anne asked, "What do you think?"

"It's different." was all he could manage to say at that point.

As he looked at all the changes—none of which he particularly liked—he was not sure how to tell her that he wanted his house put back the way he had it, but instead, he simply said nothing and accepted his newly remodeled house.

While Anne made herself at home in the kitchen, she talked nonstop about what new furniture they needed to buy and how they could make better use of the allotted space. This one-sided conversation went on during the whole meal preparation. Flutter found himself tuning her words out, but she always demanded his attention whenever she asked a question and wanted a response.

Anne finished preparing the meal and set the table to make it look inviting. Flutter had to admit that this was a nice touch and that it was nice to have a home-cooked meal prepared by someone else for a change. However, the scenario at the dinner table was no different than that in the kitchen during meal prep. She talked while serving the plates, during the meal, after the meal, and upon clearing the table. One good thing he could honestly say about Anne was that she was a fairly good cook, but then he found out that he was expected to tell her only good things after every bite.

"What do you think of my famous chicken?" and "Do you like the way I prepared the green beans?" and "Do you think the squash needs a little more bacon drippings?" were just a few examples.

He always answered in the affirmative as he was sure that it was not a good idea to tell her that while he loved fried chicken, four pieces was too many; that the green beans were a little too salty for his liking, and that the squash was not a favorite vegetable (even though he did purchase them at her request).

After spending one day with Anne and Richard, Flutter knew what Charles meant by being careful. What started out to be a way to get to know Anne slowly turned into a day of surprises that he was not sure he liked. But he kept thinking about what his mother said about the Lord sending him a good woman. He was sure that the Lord knew what was best for him, and if this was the "good woman" he was destined to meet, maybe he was supposed to change his mind-set and lifestyle to suit her preferences. This was also because his mother never told him that just because you meet a woman who seems to like you doesn't mean she is the one. Since his mother never told him this fact, how was he supposed to know it?

18

As it turned out, the day of the church "date" was only the beginning for what Anne had in store for Flutter. She made sure there was some degree of interaction with him every day: whether it was bringing him lunch to his job, cooking dinner for him each night, going to church on Sundays, or simply making sure he did not have a day to spend by himself, Flutter was involved with a woman—whether he wanted to be or not.

He did not know how to proceed or *if* he wanted to proceed. Anne was not his first choice for a wife, but he didn't know what was worse: having a bossy and controlling wife or being alone for the rest of his life. He never realized that simply having a woman in your life in no way means that you have to marry her.

Even his friend, Charles, tried to explain to him that if he decided not to marry Anne, it did not mean that he wouldn't meet another woman more suitable to him. However, in Flutter's mind, true love only comes once in a lifetime; and his true love, Lily, had already come and gone.

For the next few days, Flutter thought about life with Anne and her son, Richard. This marriage would mean he would be an instant father. *But how could I be a father when I don't even know how to be a husband?*

For the first time in his life, he sought the help from the Lord; and he actually said a prayer out loud, asking the Lord to tell him what he should do. Not really knowing how to start his prayer, he began the only way he knew how.

"My Father, which art in heaven, hallowed be thy name. Lord, I need your help. I have met this woman named Anne, and I think I should marry her but I am not sure. She is not Lily, and I do not love her like I still love Lily. Lord, I do not know what to do. Please help me. What should I do? Should I ask her to marry me? Is she the woman my mother told me I would meet? Lord, I need your guidance."

At the end of his prayer, all he could do was stay on his knees and hope that the Lord would see his anguish and tell him what he needed to do. That night, his dreams started earlier than usual. As with his dreams most nights, Lily was at the forefront.

At the beginning of his dream, Lily was there smiling at him and telling him she loved him. Somewhere in the middle, however, Lily disappeared and Anne appeared. When he woke up from his sleep and dream, he only remembered the parts featuring Anne. The two of them were happy in his dream, and he was a good father to Richard. He was also a good father to Jennifer and Carl, the children they had together. *Has the Lord answered my prayer? Does this mean that I am to marry Anne and be happy in a marriage with a woman I am not in love with?* It seemed so clear to him then, and he knew what he had to do.

During lunch break, Anne was there at her usual time. She brought Flutter tuna sandwiches, french fries, homemade cookies, and her freshly squeezed lemonade. He had to admit that he liked the special treatment. After he finished eating lunch, he asked Anne to go to his house that night at seven so they could talk. "Richard and I will be there with bells on," was her response while smiling the whole time.

"Would it be possible that you could find someone to watch Richard tonight?"

Intrigued by this request, she hesitated for a while but then later agreed.

Anne arrived on time as usual. She was anxious to hear what Flutter had to say to her. He asked her to come in and have a seat on the newly reupholstered sofa in his living room. There were no questions on Anne's part, only eager compliance because she wanted Flutter to get on with what she was hoping he would ask her. It took a little while for the words to form in his mouth, but he did notice that he was not perspiring and that his heart wasn't beating faster than normal. He only experienced these sensations when he was around Lily.

Instead of outright asking Anne to marry him, Flutter started the conversation with reasons why they should get married, but what he was actually doing was convincing *himself* that it was the right thing to do. Before he could convince himself any further, Anne jumped up from her seat, grabbed his neck, and emphatically said yes. He didn't understand that this proposal was what Anne had planned the first time she laid eyes on him in the grocery store.

That night, before Anne left an engaged woman, she had already decided that they would marry in one month and that she and her son, Richard, would begin moving in immediately. Flutter agreed mainly because he didn't know he had an equal say in the planning of this impending marriage. The wedding was going to be small, and Anne strongly "suggested" that he not invite his family since she had not met them yet. This felt off to Flutter, but again, he said nothing.

"Maybe we can go and visit them after the wedding," he offered.

"We'll see."

The next day at work, Flutter asked Charles to be his best man, and although he had some reservations, he said yes.

"I told you long ago that she wanted you, and you didn't listen. Of course, I will be your best man. I have to protect you," Charles told him with a smile on his face that turned to an extremely serious look after a few minutes.

19

It seemed like only yesterday that Flutter became engaged and today it was his wedding day. He did not like not having any of his family at his wedding. The only familiar faces that brought him solace on this supposed happy occasion were those of his best man, Charles, and his wife. Charles kept asking him right up to the beginning of the ceremony if he was sure this was what he wanted to do, but Flutter always responded with "Yes, I think the Lord has sent Anne to me."

Everything about this day had been planned by Anne with little to no input from him. (He did get to choose his suit, which was basically the only one he owned.) They had a simple ceremony, but every detail had been decided by Anne alone. They got married in the small church where they went on their so-called first date. Anne made sure that she and her son became members before the upcoming ceremony and that the preacher knew what words she wanted him to say. She decided that the vows she was to repeat out loud let everyone know that they would be equal partners and that the words *honor* and *obey* were omitted. Flutter did not even know enough to ask why she made the changes.

As soon as the words *I do* were said by them both, it seemed that a dark cloud entered the room—which meant that things would probably go straight to worse, skipping bad altogether. While it was evident that Anne was happy about becoming Mrs. Jeremy Bernard Toliver, it was also becoming very evident that Flutter was not going to be happy living with her. It was also becoming more apparent to him that his role as the man in the family was diminishing probably because she had decided that he was never going to have that role to begin with.

After a brief and small reception at the church, the newlyweds went back to their home and began their lives as a new family. What started out as a man finding his soul mate in every aspect of his life turned into one landing himself in a prison of sorts with no way to be released or pardoned.

That night, the newly married couple became husband and wife in every sense of the word; but strangely enough, Flutter's thoughts on his wedding night were of Lily and not of his wife. Even his dreams had not changed: they were of him and Lily sharing a kiss. When he woke up the next morning, he was frustrated because even though he was now married to someone other than Lily, his thoughts and dreams were still of her.

20

Flutter's married life was nothing like he thought it was going to be: he was told what to do, what to eat, when to come and go, how to dress, and even if and when he could go and see his family. He felt more like a child than a husband and man of the house. His only consolations were the several times he talked to Charles at work and the infrequent times he was allowed to go out with Charles to a sporting event. His workplace had also become his refuge since Anne no longer brought him lunch every day like she used to. Come to think of it, she stopped the first Monday after the wedding. Flutter wondered why.

Six months had passed since Flutter had become a married man, but his family still had not met his wife and stepson all because she was not ready to meet them. However, he made the decision to go to Parwell and see his family after work on Friday. After he let Anne know of his plans, she quickly reminded him that she had already made plans for them for the weekend but that if he wanted to go to Parwell instead, it was fine with her.

But, of course, by then, Flutter had already been married long enough to know that this statement could not be taken at face value and that he was supposed to cancel his plans to go with her and Richard. But to her surprise, Flutter did not change his mind but told her that he would indeed be going to Parwell and would be back late Sunday night. He was not sure how she would respond to his "defiant" response, but he stood his ground for the first time in their marriage.

To his amazement, she did not argue with him or tell him that he could not go to Parwell, but he knew what the ramifications were going to be upon his return. But he did not dwell on that. Instead he focused on how for a whole weekend, he would be able to be in a place where he could reflect on his life, see his family, and, more importantly, see and (hopefully) talk to the only woman he was still dreaming about.

With this conversation under his belt, Flutter spent the next two days happy knowing that he would be leaving his jail cell of a home if only for a weekend and gain the tranquility in his life that he so missed. The designated Friday came, and Flutter left during his lunch hour without telling his wife. He was sure that she would not find out since she no longer brought him lunch. He merely wanted to get an early start on thinking happy thoughts and enjoying his drive to Parwell.

On his drive to his family home, Flutter had decided that if he did not see Lily on this visit, he would still be in the same town close to her. He also thought about the big things that had happened in the last few years: he thought about his school days, his first encounter with Lily, his decision to join the navy, his injury while serving in the navy, and most importantly, his seeing Lily prepare to marry another man. *Oh, how my life would be much different if only I had known how to court the woman of my dreams back then!*

21

What a nice day to drive home! Flutter thought. The weather was good, and he felt good. And as bad as it sounds, he also felt good because he was not with his own family. As he pulled into the driveway of his family home, he sat in his truck for a while, taking in the scenery and thinking about memories of him growing up in this house.

He smiled thinking about the time his sisters, Beth and Janie, cooked dinner by themselves for their parents' anniversary. He was in charge of the decorations, so he hung blue and white balloons throughout the house and newspaper streamers in the dining room. The decorations did look good, he had to admit.

The meal was good as well. His sisters decided to have chicken-fried steak, mashed potatoes with gravy, collard greens, homemade rolls, and sweet potato pies. They spent all day planning and cooking their respective dishes. They all had a wonderful meal and a great time celebrating his parents' anniversary. There was good food and laughter in the midst of a happy family of people who visibly loved each other.

This memory brought back other happy ones, and it made him feel good inside. Flutter realized that all his childhood memories were at home with his family and not at school. However, the one memory he had at school—the one he treasured the most—was the first time he saw Lily. This memory was etched into his mind as he thought about this first encounter. He thought about the color of the dress she was wearing, the way her hair blew in the wind, and the way she smiled at him. While this memory of Lily made him think about all his other memories with Lily, he became sad because they made him realize that he was not married to her, which was his heart's greatest desire. This realization brought him back to the present and to where he was at the moment.

These memories, however, also made him think that he needed to speak with his parents about his current situation. While he was a grown man with a family, he needed some guidance from his mother and father. *Life is funny*, thought Flutter. He never remembered a time in his childhood when he outwardly sought his parents' advice, but now that he was an adult, all he could think about was going to his parents for guidance.

22

Everyone was glad to see Jeremy. His sisters and their families quickly came over when they got the word he was in town. They all commented on how he had changed and grown into a handsome man. It had been almost a year since he had last seen his family, and he noticed they all had changed as well—especially his father, who was visibly in poor health.

The running of the farm was virtually being done by his brothers-in-law, and his mother's time was now mostly taken up by the caring for his father.

"Flutter, we would have written you, but we did not know where to write to you," his mother said. He felt so funny after his mother said this. The realization that his father was not doing well and that no one knew how to contact him really sank in, in that moment. "I am sorry about that. I will leave you with all my contact information before I leave," he responded.

Flutter was not sure how to even bring up the subject of his life considering what he knew then of his family's circumstances. He heard about what had happened since his last visit and what his sisters and their families were doing each day to take care of his parents. While his mother was in good health, or so she seemed to be, he could see that she had begun to outwardly age (most likely due to the added assistance she was giving his father).

That night, after everyone had gone to bed, Flutter was sitting out on the porch looking at the night sky when he heard his mother come outside and join him.

"I knew you would be out here," she said. What is going on with my baby boy?"

"Where do I begin? Earlier today, I was thinking about the fifteenth anniversary dinner that we prepared for you and Daddy all those years ago."

"Yes, I remember that. That was a wonderful dinner," his mother said with a smile on her face. As she was still smiling, Flutter began telling her all about his life and the choices he had made. Her smile slowly wavered, but she did not interrupt her son while he was pouring out his heart to her; she knew that he needed her to listen and to comfort him at this moment. The mother and son spent the next four hours talking and listening to each other. Flutter had forgotten how compassionate and understanding his mother was—even to this day.

During their conversation (which was mostly Flutter telling his mother about what he acknowledged as his mistake), his mother said something that he would never forget.

She said to him in a whisper of a voice, "Son, life is funny. As we go through it, there will be many decisions that we all will have to make. You must remember that before you make any decision, you must ask the Lord to guide your thoughts and steps. Flutter, he will hear you, and he will answer your prayers.

But always know that the Lord will never lead us astray. He knew—before you did—that you would marry Anne, so you have to think that maybe this was destined to happen. If you truly believe that this marriage was a mistake, then ask the Lord to help you in correcting it. Maybe the Lord was telling you to get on with your life, and you thought that meant to marry Anne."

Flutter was amazed that his mother did not make him feel bad during this conversation. That day and the next two were the happiest he'd ever had since his marriage. When it was time for him to go, he said his good-byes and remembered to leave his home address and house phone number as well as his work telephone number with his mother. Her parting words were "Flutter, remember our talk the other night." His father and sisters looked puzzled, but no one asked what she meant by this statement.

With new insight into his life and his family, Flutter slowly drove down the street; but before he took the long ride back home, he decided to drive by Lily's house. He had not thought about Lily during this visit as much as he guessed he would, but he had to admit that she was indeed one of the reasons he decided to make this visit. Parking at his self-designated spot in front of Lily's house, he drove up, turned off the engine, and just sat in his truck now parked in front of the house. He would not go to the door, but if by chance or for whatever reason she happened to come outside, he would indeed talk with her.

After sitting here for about thirty minutes, he decided that there was probably no chance he was going to see her that day, so he started his truck and began his trip back to Dallas. As he drove down the town street, marked by Parwell townspeople doing their chores, he decided to stop at the well-known town grocery store to get some travel food.

He walked into the store and headed for the aisle with the snacks he was looking for. He did not pay attention to the people already in the store when he walked in. He then selected the items he wanted to purchase. Turning around to leave, he noticed a pregnant woman walking toward him. The closer she got to him, the more familiar she looked. It was a noticeably pregnant Lily. He remained rooted in his spot while she stopped in her tracks.

"Hello, Lily," finally came from his mouth.

"Hello, Flutter," she responded.

A few more seconds passed before Flutter commented, "I see you have news."

"Yes, I am expecting a baby in two months," Lily replied.

"I am happy for you and your husband."

"Thank you. How are you doing in the big city?"

"Well, I am married now, and my wife has a son. So I guess I am a father too."

Lily did not speak for a few seconds, and she then replied, "I am happy for you too."

It was evident that both of them wanted to say something to each other, but neither one knew how to begin. Finally, Lily broke the silence.

"Flutter, I think about you all the time. I know I shouldn't, but I can't help it. This should be our baby."

Flutter felt his face heat up, and he replied with words from his heart.

"I know. I think about you all the time too. I have to admit when I came down here, I was hoping to see you. I parked in front of your house earlier today hoping to see you. When I didn't see you at your house, I just gave up thinking I would see you this trip. I feel just as you do, and I always will."

The two just stood in the store and stared at each other until Lily said that it was time for her to finish her errands. Flutter wished her well and bid her good-bye.

On his drive back to Dallas, he thought about his mother's encouraging words, his father's failing health, and, of course, the woman he loved. In that moment, he started praying.

23

Just as Flutter anticipated, Anne made his life difficult for the next few weeks. He explained to her that he needed to see his family and told her that he was glad he went home. Surprisingly, he was able to get his message across to her and make her understand that she would not come between him and his family. However, when it came to everything else in his life, he could not and would not stand up to her. Deciding that this marriage was his fate, he simply made it through each day in the easiest way he could manage to keep the peace.

It was no surprise to him when Anne told him she was pregnant. He tried to be excited with this news, but while he was happy with the prospect that he was going to be a father for real this time, all he kept thinking about was how he should be having this baby with Lily. Over the next couple of months, he heard from his mother frequently via mail and telephone. He often asked about his father, and every time, she just told him that his health was further deteriorating. "I think it is finally time that you all meet my family. We will be down in a week," he told his mother.

On the scheduled day of their trip to Parwell, Anne woke up with severe nausea. It was evident that she could not make the trip with him, so with her approval, Flutter took Richard with him. As he drove into the driveway of his parents' home, he did not see any movement outside or inside of the house.

When he went inside the house, no one was there. He saw a note from his mother telling him that his father had to be taken to the hospital and that he was to meet them there. He jumped back into his truck and headed for the hospital. Once inside, he found out that his father had been diagnosed with pneumonia and was in the ICU.

Making his way to the right floor in the right wing of the hospital took him less than five minutes. Flutter saw his family in the waiting room, and everyone there greeted him with hugs and some tears. His mother told him that his father's lungs were weak but that he was stable. The doctor thought that he would make a complete recovery, but apparently it was going to have to be a few days before he could go home. Flutter felt relief and happiness that his father's illness was not life threatening.

After some brief introductions, his mother asked him to go back to the house and get some things for his father. He was happy to comply. He left Richard with his mother and sisters, knowing that he would be fine with them. On his way to his truck, he saw Lily standing by the nursery window, peering through it. He walked over to her and stood beside her. She looked at him and smiled. She then showed him her two-day-old son.

"He's beautiful," Flutter told her.

"Thank you. But what are you doing here, in town?"

"My father is in the hospital in ICU, but he is going to be all right. What is your son's name?"

"His name is Bernard James Fields. His father and I both liked the name Bernard, and he did not want a junior. So we decided on that name."

Flutter did not bring up the fact that Bernard was also his middle name, but he was sure that Lily was somehow aware of this and that this was her way of telling him she still loved him.

"Where is his father? I know he is proud of his newborn son."

"Yes, he is. He went to pick up his parents so they could see their new grandson."

Flutter went on to tell Lily that his wife was also pregnant and that he was happy about that. Lily smiled at Flutter and he smiled back at her. However, after a few short minutes, he knew that it was time to say good-bye. So he wished her and her new family well and went on to accomplish his task. He hated to walk away, but he knew it was the right thing to do. Though he could not see Lily as he walked away, he felt Lily's eyes on him until he got in the elevator. Alone in the elevator, he exclaimed, "Oh, how I love that woman!"

The next few days in Parwell, Flutter helped his mother with chores around the house and making sure that his father was getting better. Before it was time for him to go back to Dallas, his father was released from the hospital. He made sure his parents were taken care of. Then he and Richard drove back to Dallas.

24

Over the last ten years, a lot has happened in the Toliver household. Flutter was now a true father of nine-year-old Stephen Bernard Toliver. He often thought about the dream he had before he got married. In the dream, he saw himself happily married and with two children, a girl and a boy.

He realized that dreams do not always have bearing on real life because he was really unhappy in his marriage, and he was the father of only one biological child: Anne had suffered some complications during delivery, and they were told that she could not have any more children. He was also aware that his middle name, Bernard, was now his son's but that it was also the first name of Lily's son. For now, only Flutter knew this fact.

Sad to say that also during this time, Flutter's father passed away, and his mother was now living alone in his childhood home. His sisters and their husbands made sure she ate and the house was maintained. It seemed as though since her husband was no longer around, she no longer had interest in anything else but going to church. Tuesday night Bible study, Thursday night choir rehearsal, and two Sunday church services were added to her Wednesday prayer services. Flutter made sure he spoke to his mother on the telephone at least three times a week and visited her once a week.

Whenever he went home to visit his mother, though, he somehow ended up running into Lily: whether it was at a store, at the founders' day parade, at the library, or even at the cemetery, they would always happened to bump into each other. They spoke pleasantries; but each of them knew there was still a deep-seated love underneath spouses, children, and cities. These chance meetings were *never* planned (unlike in the case with Anne) but, nevertheless, welcomed by both.

On one of his many trips home to visit his mother, he decided to stay over and attend a Sunday morning church service. As they walked into the building, he noticed that it was a particularly crowded service and the only seats available were those in the last pew. When they sat down, he noticed that the people they were sitting next to were Lily and her family. Of course, he was sitting next to Lily and because the seating arrangements were close, their hands touched as though they'd been holding hands. There was no way to move to provide a bit of distance between them, but this seemed to please Lily.

When the church service was over, Lily spoke with Flutter's mother and introduced Flutter to her husband as an old classmate. But deep down, he still hoped that is not all he really was and would ever be to her. Octavia knew her son loved Lily, but she never broached the subject with him. In fact, she herself had always been partial to Lily and always treated her like her own daughter.

All the chance encounters over the years seemed to make it that much harder for both Flutter and Lily to hide their true feelings for each other. Flutter had to admit that he looked forward to his weekly trips home not only because he got to see his mother and the rest of his family; but also because he got to see Lily, even if only for a brief moment (seeing her was always on his trip agenda).

So who would believe that on one brisk autumn day while he was on one of his many errands for Anne that he would run into Lily in Dallas? She explained that she was on her way to see a specialist whom her husband had visited a week before. Flutter, in turn, said that he was on his way to pick up some medication for his wife. After discussing their mutual health-related errands for their respective spouses, the two decided to indulge their feelings and actually have lunch together. They went to a small cafeteria that Flutter frequented to be alone.

Unlike countless times before when Flutter was around Lily, he had no problem speaking his mind on this day. They talked about what could have been and being married to other people. It seemed that both of their spouses were suffering from illnesses that had taken a toll on their lives and on those of their families. They couldn't help but dwell on how their lives were going in much the same way and how they kept running into each other all these years.

One thing was for sure: this was the best time Flutter had had in a while. Not wanting to but knowing they had to, the non-couple said their good-byes, hesitating walking away from each other. They both knew and probably thought at the same time about where they would see each other the next time around.

25

During the next ten years, Flutter experienced and lived through many more changes in his life. First of all, his beloved mother, Octavia, died (from natural causes). She had not been sick. She had been living fine, going on her weekly church visits until she passed away in her sleep on a Sunday morning. At her prior request, she had a tasteful service at her church and was buried next to her beloved husband, Jacob. It seemed as though the entire town of Parwell was in attendance at the funeral.

While it was a sad occasion, it was still a joyous time because everyone who attended had wonderful stories about Octavia Toliver. This made her family happy and the loss easier to accept. Lily made a point of coming to the funeral and paying her respects. She and Octavia had become very close, and she felt like Octavia was her second mother. And while she felt close to Flutter's mother and his sisters, especially Beth, like they were part of her own family, she never felt like Flutter was anything but the love of her life.

During his many visits home to see his mother (always alone at his wife's request and insistence), Flutter and Lily had many chance meetings that they always enjoyed. On several occasions, he actually had the opportunity of meeting Lily's son, Bernard. He couldn't help thinking, *This could have been my son and my wife.* The boy was about a year older than his own son and looked so much like his mother, Octavia, that he could easily be mistaken as his son.

The two lovebirds had gotten to really know each other on these unplanned encounters, and they both still felt the love they experienced as teenagers, almost thirty years ago. Flutter also could not help thinking about all the similarities in their lives: their spouses suffering from an illness, the (close) ages of their sons, and both boys sharing his middle name. In one of his conversations with Lily, he found out that her husband had been diagnosed with colon cancer. She too had become the decision maker in her household with everything.

Also, one of the biggest changes in Flutter's life now involved his wife, Anne. Her health had become increasingly worse as well, and it was a burden on Flutter. He tried his best to help her in every way he could—from taking control in the raising of their children to doing the household chores. Anne was in bed most of the time if she was not in the hospital for some procedure. But one thing was for sure: she was no longer in control of their lives. *What a way to be the man in your own house!*

His two young boys had now turned into young men with their own lives. Although Flutter always talked about his sons as though they were still those little boys he raised mostly by himself. "I'm so proud of my boys," he often said. One thing he made sure of was that his sons got to know their grandmother before she passed. His older son, Richard, was now in the navy, which made Flutter happy while his younger son, Stephen, was in college studying to become a lawyer.

His sons would always say to him, "Daddy, we are going to take care of you for a change." They were not aware of their father's loneliness. If only they knew that while he loved them, he yearned to be with a woman other than their mother.

26

It was about 6:30 a.m. on a cold winter's day in November 1983 when Flutter's telephone rang. His first thought was that the hospital was calling to tell him that Anne's condition had taken a turn for the worse. But he thought that this couldn't be as this was only to be an overnight hospital stay for early morning tests, so he was just imagining the worst. Reluctantly, in a low voice, he answered the telephone. He realized that the voice on the other end was that of his sister, Beth.

"Good morning, Flutter. Sorry I am calling so early, but I knew you would want to know what happened to Lily's family late last night—y'know since she is just like one of the family."

His heart began to pound in much the same way it always did when he was around Lily, but this time, it felt different: he felt strangely terrified at what his sister was about to say.

Beth was right. He indeed wanted to know about everything that Lily was going through, but she had no idea why he was still as concerned about her as he had been for his entire life.

"What happened, Beth?"

"The way Mr. Andrews—you know, the repairman who works at Murford's Car Garage and Gas Station—explained it to me was it was a tragic accident. He said that Lily's husband, James, had some sort of an attack late last night and that Lily was not at home because she had gone to pick up his medicine at the drugstore. So her son, Bernard, who was at home at the time, decided to drive his father to the hospital when he lost control of the car and ran into an embankment.

The car caught on fire and burned up, but both of them were thrown from the car during the collision, before the fire started. Mr. Andrews said her husband and son were both declared dead on arrival. He kept saying what a terrible accident it was."

Flutter was quiet because he could not speak. He pictured everything Beth was saying in his head, and tears began to flow.

"Have you seen Lily?"

"No, I am going over there later this morning. I have been trying to call her, but there is no answer. I knew you would want to know since she was a good friend of yours, and we all really care about her."

His sister was right about his feelings for Lily, but while she knew about how her brother felt about Lily, she had no idea how deep his feelings were. Before saying it out loud, he had already made his mind up to go see Lily as soon as he got Anne home from the hospital.

At exactly 12:00 p.m., Flutter was in his truck and on his way to Parwell, Texas. He had no idea what he would say to Lily, but he knew that he had to be close to her. What was approximately an hour-and-a-half trip had turned into an hour's drive. It didn't take as long for Flutter to reach the main thoroughfare in Parwell. He did not know where to look for her first, but it suddenly came to him. He then made a left at the next light and headed for the cemetery. When he got closer to the small cemetery, he saw Lily kneeling in front of her mother's grave.

As he walked up to her, he heard her say, "Mother, I have lost my husband and son, and I need you to take care of them. I have already asked the Lord to give me strength to accept what happened. I am trying my best not to be angry—" Then she started crying.

Flutter put his hand on her shoulder; and she turned around, got up, and tightly hugged him. She began crying out loud and holding on to her dear friend.

"Flutter, somehow I knew you would be here. My family is gone and I am alone. I can't blame anyone, and I know the Lord does not make mistakes. Thank you for coming."

"Lily, you know I couldn't stay away. I can't imagine what you are going through right now, but I am here for you. What can I do to help you?"

"Please help me make the arrangements."

"Of course I will help you. You didn't even have to ask," was his response. Then they both stood there talking and looking at each other for the next few hours.

27

The funeral took place exactly one week after that horrid car accident. Flutter remained by Lily's side as much as he could while still looking after his wife, Anne. But when he could not be there for Lily, he made sure that his sisters were with her as well as a few neighbors and friends. At Lily's request, the joint service for her husband and her son was quick but poignant. The pastor said wonderful things about Lily and her family and about how she was a big part of the Parwell community.

At the conclusion of the funeral service, the onlookers slowly walked away, and Lily just sat in the green chair under the green tent and watched as they lowered her husband and then her son into the darkness of the ground. Flutter was there holding her hand the entire time, but when he saw the tears trickle down her face, he cried with her.

Later that day, after all the well wishers had paid their respects, offered condolences, and prepared food, Lily and Flutter were left alone. Lily talked about the loss of her family and told him how much it meant to her that he was there for her.

"Jeremy, how did you explain this to your wife?"

"I told her my friend needed me and I was going to help in any way I could."

She noticed that he never mentioned that his "friend" was a woman, especially one he loved and would do anything for.

The day turned into night, and Flutter realized that it was time for him to leave. "Thank you, Flutter, for all you have done. I will never forget your kindness and the love you showed me," Lily commented. Strangely enough, as Flutter turned to leave the house, Lily said something that he could not believe.

"Flutter, I will never forget my husband and son. It is going to take me a long time to accept the fact that they are gone from my life. I keep telling myself the Lord had a plan for me that I do not understand yet, but I truly believe that plan includes you. I am not asking you to do anything or say anything. Just know that however long it may take, this time, I will be here waiting for you. Yes, I know you are married and you have responsibilities. I am not asking for you to leave your wife and family, but I will wait for you. If we are meant to be together, then we will be."

Not sure how to respond (or even *if* he should respond), he simply grabbed her hand, kissed it, and whispered in her ear, "You are an amazing woman, Lily. Everything you are going through is basically my fault. If only I had not taken you and our relationship for granted, I do believe we would have been married now with our own children. I do not know what the future holds for me and Anne, but I cannot leave her, especially now that she is sick. I will be a good husband because I believe that is what the Lord wants me to do. All I can do is take one day at a time."

He wanted to kiss her, but he knew this was not the right moment or the right occasion. He thought, *Is there ever going to be a right time for us?* So for now, he settled on saying, "Lily, I will always love you, and I hope that we will have our time. But only the Lord knows if that will ever happen." With that, they hugged each other, and Flutter turned slowly and reluctantly left.

28

Life for Jeremy Bernard Toliver in Dallas changed more each day. His older son, Richard, was now out of the navy and was married to a woman he met while he was stationed in Florida. She seemed to be a nice enough young woman and appeared to genuinely love Richard. They had settled into a small home, which was about thirty miles from Flutter and Anne's home, and had one child and were expecting another one any day. His wife, Susan, had no living family, so she really took to Anne and Flutter as her mother and father. Since Anne was sick most of the time, Susan was happy to help care for her when she needed.

Flutter's younger son, Stephen, had now graduated from law school and was working in a law firm in downtown Dallas. He and his longtime girlfriend, Chrystal (also an attorney), recently got married. They met in the last year of college and continued dating throughout law school. Everyone liked Chrystal and knew that whenever they decided to start a family, she would be a good mother. Anne seemed to like both of her sons' choice in women (which was good because she did not really have any close friends to speak to).

Through the years, Anne suffered many attacks of various natures that caused her to have lung problems and, consequently, difficulty breathing. She was weak and unable to perform any household chores, such as cooking and cleaning, and her few outings were now limited to trips to the doctor's office or the hospital. By this time, Flutter had been going to most places alone, even church; but he honestly did not mind.

Her weak lungs had necessitated her to use an oxygen tank every day. It also seemed that she became weaker by the day. The doctors had discussed the possibility of her maybe having a lung transplant, but Anne said no (which meant that at some point, her lungs would simply stop working and the oxygen would not be sufficient). She was aware that her decision ultimately would mean death, so she prepared herself and her family for what was to be. But though Flutter had always been a good husband to her, she never knew of his secret yearning to be with another.

Since the funeral for Lily's husband and her son, Flutter had been home at least once a week to check on his sisters and their families. The family home was now being occupied by Beth's oldest son, Jonathan Wayne, and his family. It was Octavia's wish that the home would stay in the family, and this seemed like the perfect fit.

The town of Parwell had grown over the years to a bustling metropolis with many new families making their homes here. Some of the old businesses had been bought out by larger companies or were being run by second- or third-generation family members. It always amazed Flutter as he made his once-a-week trip home how much this small town had changed. The church, like so many businesses, was now under the charge of the grandson of the minister whom his mother loved so much. He even occasionally came down on a Sunday just to hear Rev. Butler speak to his congregation.

There were also now two more high schools in addition to the one he was so familiar with during his high school days. On one of his many trips home, he made a point of driving by his old high school, which looked a little different now due to some new renovations; and to his surprise, Lily was there sitting on a bench in front of the building. Of course, he had to stop and say hello to an old friend. He was still amazed at how they still had these chance encounters and still found much to talk about.

As he got out of the car, he noticed some of those all-too-familiar feelings he used to get whenever he was around Lily. He knew what the heart palpitations and sweaty palms meant after all of these years, but unlike what he experienced as a young boy, he relished the opportunities to see and speak with the girl who had not changed; she still had those prominent dimples, beautiful now-gray-streaked hair, and shapely legs that he fell in love with all those years ago.

Lily often talked about how her family was no longer in her life but still in her thoughts. Their conversations always ended with them talking about how different their lives would have been if only certain conversations had been had.

Flutter always took the blame for them not being together, but Lily always said to him, "Flutter, the Lord knows what is best for us. In due time, if he wills it, we will be together." With that, they changed the subject and talked about how much the city had changed since they were kids. As their conversations came to an end, the two simply hugged each other gently and knew that there would indeed be a next time.

29

While at work one January day in 1993, Flutter received one of those troubling phone calls about Anne being taken to the hospital which he seemed to get too often from his daughter-in-law, Susan. Of course, he rushed right over and was greeted by his family. The doctor came out to speak to everyone and basically said what had been known for a long time: Anne's lungs were just too weak, and it was just a matter of time. While everyone was sad at the news, she had prepared them well.

Just as the doctor had said, two days later, Anne died, her family by her bedside. Flutter felt odd because even though he was not happy with her, he never wished for anything bad to happen to her. Having known that this day was approaching, Flutter and everyone in the family had already discussed with her what type of service she wanted, and everything had already been planned.

The service was held on a cold and dreary January day. It was held in the church where they had gotten married and was officiated by the nephew of the pastor that married them all those years ago. Many nice things were said about Anne and her dedication to the church. There were not many people outside of the family members at the home-going service; but Flutter's friend, Charles, and his wife had made sure they were there.

At the end of the service, as the family followed the casket out into the cold, Flutter noticed a woman dressed in black and sitting in the last seat of the back pew. He turned to look at her and noticed that it was Lily. No one else noticed her there, but he assumed one of his sisters had told her of Anne's passing.

She did not follow them to the gravesite or come back to the house with the others in the family. Flutter did not see her anymore that day, but it made him feel good to see her for that brief moment.

Months after Anne's funeral, Flutter made the decision to retire from work at the end of the year. He discussed it with his family, and they were happy for him. He had no actual plans, but one thing he intended to do was to contact Lily. Thoughts of her had taken over his mind since he saw her at the funeral though he had not spoken to her as of yet.

As his retirement drew nearer, he made a point of calling Lily, telling her about his plans, and asking her to attend a small get-together that his family was planning. She agreed to come and told him that she would call him the day before she was to leave to let him know what time to expect her.

He had not felt this happy in a long time, but he knew his happiness had always been because of Lily. As promised, the day before his retirement celebration, Lily called Flutter with news of her arrival. By this time, however, Flutter was taking the trash out, and his son Richard answered the phone. Lily explained that she was an old high school friend of Jeremy's and had been invited to the party. She went on to explain that she would be arriving at around 1:00 p.m.

"Could you please tell your father when I will be arriving," Lily asked. Without hesitation, Richard replied, "I do understand that my father invited you to the party we are giving him, but it is strictly for family. It would probably be best that you not attend as space and food will be limited. However, thank you for calling."

With that, Richard hung up the phone and did not relay the message to his father. Lily was not sure what to think about the comments she just heard. She decided that it was best that she not attend and not to call Flutter to explain. The last thing she wanted to do was cause a problem in Flutter's family. But as the day went on, Flutter kept waiting for a phone call from Lily. Not knowing what to do, he just assumed she had decided to just come to the party without calling him beforehand. It never occurred to him to call her.

When everyone except Lily showed up, Flutter got antsy. He still never thought to call her to see if there was anything wrong. In many ways, he was still that shy boy who was afraid to speak to the one girl who captured his heart. And because he essentially had not been allowed to think or act for himself when he was married, he was at a loss. So the day came and went, and he did not know what to make of Lily not having kept her word. Not once did he entertain the idea of outside forces keeping them apart.

30

As luck would have it (perhaps the bad kind), Lily did indeed try and call Flutter on several more occasions; but to her surprise and utter frustration, someone other than Flutter always answered the phone. It seemed that his sons and their wives had decided that it was not proper for their father to be speaking with another woman so soon after his late wife's death, so they had all agreed that they would intercept all calls and discourage her once and for all.

Finally, after many attempts, Lily got the message and never called Flutter again. She did not want to come between Flutter and his family, but she always hoped that she would see Flutter when he came home. But just as the communication between the star-crossed lovers had seemingly stopped, so have the weekly Parwell visits. When Lily did not make an appearance at his retirement celebration, almost a year ago, Flutter took that to mean that she did not want to see him anymore.

What started as a happy occasion with his retirement and the possibility of finally being with Lily had turned into sadness and the slow demise of a relatively young man. His children did not know what to make of this sudden change in their father. They simply surmised that he missed their mother.

As the months progressed, Flutter's health declined with no visible cause. The doctors were baffled at his condition and were at a loss as to how to treat their patient. They were also not sure what medications to prescribe to him. His sisters and his children were visibly concerned and helpless.

Even though Parwell had grown in population, one thing had remained: word travels fast among neighbors and friends. Lily had been told by Beth just how sick he was and that the doctors did not know how to treat him. Lily was upset at the news, so she made a point of going to Dallas that afternoon to see Flutter.

When she arrived at the hospital, she found her way to where he was, and she noticed everyone in his family around him. She could see him from where she was standing outside of the room. He did not know she was there. She could see all of the tubes coming from all over his body, and tears began flowing down her cheeks. Not wanting to intrude, she left the hospital.

That night she prayed not only that he recover but also that they be finally together. Hoping her prayers would not be too late, she prayed all night and thought about them being together. But as always, only time would tell.

31

No sooner had she gotten out of bed than she heard a knock on her door. She could not imagine who would come to see her so early in the morning. She opened the door, and her heart skipped a beat. It was Beth. She came over to tell Lily the latest news about Flutter.

"I just received a call from my nephew. He let me know that they had made the decision to take him off life support in the morning. It was a hard decision for them, but they could not stand to see him like this anymore."

Unable to speak, Lily fell to her knees and began crying uncontrollably. Beth tried to console her as best as she could, understanding why she was so distraught.

The next morning, after a night of not wanting to or not being able to sleep, Lily decided to go to Dallas and see her Flutter one last time. She knew that he would know she was there even though he was unconscious. So knowing this was what she needed to do, Lily got in her car and went off on her last trip and journey to see the love of her life.

On the way to the hospital, she thought about all those memories of Flutter she had over the years and found herself smiling and crying at the same time. But the closer she got to Dallas, the sadder she became and the more uncontrollable her crying got—so much so that she had to pull over on the side of the road to calm down.

After about thirty minutes, Lily decided that it was probably best if she did not go and see Flutter, for various reasons. But the main one being that she could not control her unrelenting tears and immense sadness, and she knew that she could not explain that to his family. So at this moment, she decided to turn her car around and go back home.

She slowly turned the key in her ignition because while she knew that returning home was the right thing to do, she still wanted to see her Flutter one last time. But before she could change her mind and complete her trip to Dallas, her car made the decision for her; it did not start. She could not help but think that the forces trying to keep her and Flutter apart were still at work. Now that she basically gave up, her mind was focused on getting her car started so that she could get back home.

She remembered that on two other occasions in the last two weeks, her car had not started; but she'd always been close to home or to Murt's garage, so she was able to get help. She did remember one of the mechanics at the garage telling her she needed a new starter, and she promised that she would bring her car in soon to get those repairs.

As she sat in her car, thinking about what she was going to do, she noticed from her rearview mirror a car pulling up behind her. She saw a man getting out of the car and heading toward her door. He lightly knocked on her window, and she rolled it down.

"Hello, ma'am. I noticed you sitting here and was wondering if you needed some help. Is your car on the fritz?" said this seemingly helpful man. "No need to cry, ma'am. I'm pretty good under a hood. Let's see what we have."

Before she could respond, he opened up the hood and began investigating.

"Ma'am, could you please step out of your car? I need to check your ignition."

This statement brought Lily back to reality, and she responded,

"Yes, my mechanic told me I needed a new starter. I had planned to get it fixed next week. I think that's why it won't start."

"No problem. I can jiggle a few things here and see if I can get it started so that you can at least get back home."

After a few minutes of jiggling, Lily's car started.

"Now don't stop anywhere else before you get home, and make sure you get a new starter as soon as possible."

"Thank you so much for your help. I am not sure what I was going to do. You were a Godsend," Lily responded. Her tears had stopped flowing, but her heart was still breaking—she felt every break on her way back home. When she finally pulled back in to her driveway, all she could do was sit there for a couple of hours and relive her memories.

32

The rest of that day and night, all Lily had were her memories of how they never really began. She blamed herself for the way things turned out; her anger and willingness to accept another man's proposal when her heart belonged to another resulted in this punishment. No one knew how much she was grieving, but her grief was all she had to remember the true love of her life: there had been no love letters, no pressed flowers in a book, no wedding announcement, no baby shower—nothing in the world that linked them together.

She had not heard anything from Beth, so she decided to call her and find out if Flutter had been taken off life support. Beth did not answer, so she decided to call the hospital and see if she could get some information about Flutter on her own. When she called the hospital, she told the nurse that she was Flutter's sister and that she was just calling to check on her brother. The nurse said his sons had decided to wait until 9:00 a.m. of the following day to discontinue the life support.

Lily felt happy and relieved upon hearing this news. She knew that this time, she would indeed make that trip to Dallas to see him one last time. Lily left home early not because she was anxious to see her one true love taking his last breath but because she was hoping to see him alone, even for a brief moment. She was sure that even in his state, he would feel her presence.

When she got to her car, again, it did not start; but she tried over and over again, determined to make this trip to Dallas and back home. She then decided that she would get her car repaired the minute she returned. Lily did not take this small inconvenience as a sign that she should not attempt this drive (she also did not think that maybe she should get the car checked before getting on the highway). All she could think about was seeing Flutter one last time, even though it would be as he was taking his last breath.

She was already leaving later than she wanted to because of the car episode, so of course, she had to speed to make up for lost time—in more ways than one. As Lily approached the highway, her car stalled for a brief moment. Again her only concern was getting to Dallas. Evidently, there was something wrong with her car besides the starter, but she was determined to make this trip.

Once again, she got the engine going when it stalled a second time on the on-ramp of the highway. This time, however, she could not get it to start again. She sat there trying her best not to think about getting out of the car and looking for help. Not noticing anything around her (mainly because all she could think about was her beloved, Flutter), she did not see or hear the large speeding eighteen wheeler approaching her from behind.

She heard a blaring horn of what sounded like a large truck that seemed to be getting closer and closer, but when she finally realized what was coming her way, it was too late. She knew what was about to happen to her; it was inevitable. Strangely enough, she was not afraid. She only thought, *At last, I would be with my one true love.*

Lily's car had been hit from behind, and the impact flipped her car onto the highway. It was hit several times by other cars. It took several hours for the rescue vehicles and police to control the accident and all the cars involved. News of this horrific accident somehow also made its way into the Dallas media. Everyone knew the facts reported by the media, but no names were mentioned—only that it was a lone woman who caused the accidents.

33

Lily was taken to the nearby hospital, Fairfield Memorial. This hospital was not equipped with the state-of-the-art staff and equipment, but she was getting the best treatment they could provide. While the doctors were amazed that she was still alive, they were also worried that she was not responding to anything being done to her: there were tubes in her mouth, in her nose, and in her arms. It seemed as though nothing was visible to anyone except the numerous tubes going in different parts of her body.

The doctors were all amazed that, first of all, Lily survived the accident and, second, that she remained stable. "It seems as though she has a will to live," one of her doctors commented.

Day in and day out, Lily lay in bed unresponsive to any treatment. What started out as the day of Lily being brought into the hospital after an accident she had on her way to see Flutter had turned into months of unresponsiveness, but it was still life nonetheless.

The only person that ever visited Lily was Flutter's sister Beth. Her visits started out as often as a couple of times a week but had turned as infrequent as once or twice a month. Though Lily no longer had family per se to take care of her, Beth felt like she was her sister and thought that she had to at least check on her whenever she could. Not only was she visiting Lily; but she was also visiting her brother, Flutter, who was still in the hospital in Dallas. Miraculously, when the breathing tube was removed from his mouth six months ago, he started breathing on his own. The doctors and his family were also amazed to say the least, at his will to live.

During her visits to Flutter, Beth spoke to her brother as though he could hear her; and in one conversation, she told him about Lily's accident and how she had been in the hospital these last six months. There was no response from him during these conversations, so Beth was not sure if he actually heard her words. But she always felt better when she provided him information that no one else knew. Conversely, during her visits to see Lily, she told her about Flutter's condition; and just like in his case, there was no reaction, so Beth was not sure if her words were heard or not.

These one-sided conversations with Beth continued for both Lily and Flutter for an additional two months, and almost to the same day, Lily's and Flutter's doctors had come to the conclusion that these two patients should be moved to another facility that was more equipped to care for comatose patients. Since Beth was now the family of record for Lily, all she could say was "Where is this facility, and when will she be moved?"

"Our little town is not equipped to handle long-term–care patients such as Lily, but we have contacted the doctors at the Dallas St. Paul Long-Term Care Hospital, and they say that they have two spaces available. If this meets with your approval, she can be transported there tomorrow. And because her husband was on the board of several hospitals in Dallas, her care will be free of charge."

"All right. How early will she be transported?"

"The ambulance has been scheduled for 9:30 a.m., and it will take her directly to the facility. If you would like to ride in the ambulance with her, you can."

"No, I will follow the ambulance so that after she is settled, I can go visit my brother."

With that, Lily's future (for however long that was) had been decided.

34

True to the doctor's word, the ambulance was there a little before nine thirty so that Lily could be prepared for her trip to Dallas. Beth had arrived just as they were taking her into the ambulance. After she signed the paperwork, Lily was on her way to Dallas and closer to her beloved, Flutter (even though he had no way of knowing this fact and neither did she).

Beth had tried to call her nephews earlier that morning to see how her brother was and to let them know that she would be by to see him later in the day, but she had not been able to get ahold of them. So she just assumed they had gone to the hospital to see their father.

As the ambulance backed into the emergency entrance port, attendants and nurses waiting to assist Lily met the vehicle. Beth noticed that the staff was very attentive and accommodating.

"Hello, Miss Lily. It is so good to meet you. I am Dr. Larkin, and I will be your physician while you are living here at St. Paul. We have been anxiously waiting on your arrival." The doctor then turned to Beth and asked, "Are you Miss Lily's relative?"

"Yes, she is my sister."

Beth was very impressed with the care that Lily was receiving so far, and she had not even made it to her room yet. As they rolled her down several corridors, it was evident that Lily was going to be well taken care of. They stopped in front of room 187; and Lily was slowly moved into her new home, which was very nice. There was light coming in from the window, brightening up the room.

As Beth looked out of the window, she saw the hospital garden and all the beautiful flowers. They had been arranged in such a way that you could see all the different colors and various plants throughout the whole area. There were benches strategically placed amongst the array of colors and variations of flower. She wished Lily could see her surroundings, but then she realized that if she could, she would not be here in the first place. When she thought of that alternative, she was happy to be seeing the flowers for her.

Lily was settled in her new room at around noon and a total of seven doctors and nurses had been into her room during this transition period. Beth met them all, and they made a point of getting to know her as well. She noticed that there was an empty bed across the room from Lily's.

"Will she be getting a roommate?" Beth asked one of Lily's nurses.

"Yes, she will have a roommate as soon as the family signs the transfer papers. Maybe later today," responded the nurse.

Beth thought she should wait for a while to make sure this new roommate would be acceptable.

As the nurse had said, three hours or so later, the hospital staff came in to prepare the other side of Lily's room.

"This is the last bed we had vacant in the facility, and both were filled on the same day."

"Is that unusual?"

"Yes, it is. We had a waiting list of about thirty people, and these last two beds were supposed to be assigned to two other people. Lily and her roommate were not on the list. Not sure what happened. They must be important people." The nurse smiled.

Beth heard the conversation and commotion in the hallway get louder the closer they got to Lily's room. Soon she heard a familiar voice as she saw the bed finally make its way into the room and placed in the appointed location.

As the nurses and doctors were tending to the new patient, making sure his machinery was working properly and that all of his tubes were plugged in correctly, Beth's nephews walked into the room. She then walked over to the bed of the new patient to get a closer look. It was then when she realized that this new patient was her brother, Flutter.

35

Tears began to fall down Beth's face, and she could not speak. Only she knew what her tears really meant. Her brother had confided in her many years ago about his love for Lily and how they could never seem to be together.

"Aunt Beth, what are you doing here? How did you know that Dad would be moved here today?" Flutter's older son Richard, asked.

"I didn't. I had planned to visit him later today after I got my friend settled in with her new environment."

Beth did not elaborate because she knew that her brother had not mentioned his true feelings about Lily to his children. She walked over to her brother, hugged him, and then whispered in his hear some words she knew would make him happy. "Flutter, Lily is here with you now, right across the room. If you open your eyes, you can see her all you want."

Beth started to shed more tears as she hugged her brother again. Everyone just thought she was happy to see her brother, and she was. But there was more to these tears.

"This situation just keeps getting better and better," the nurse commented. "Your friend and brother are together in the same room. Do they know each other?"

Beth chose her words carefully and replied, "We all are from the same small town." She felt this was enough information for all involved. Beth spent the rest of the day smiling, shedding tears, and silently praying for a miracle for both her brother and Lily.

As her nephews said their good-byes to their aunt and father, Beth waited until the room was quiet and all she could hear were monitors from both sides of the room. Then she prayed out loud.

"Most Gracious Father in heaven, thank you for your infinite wisdom and for finally bringing Flutter and Lily together. Lord, only you know of what they have been through all these years, but you brought them together now. Please let them be aware that their prayers have been answered and that they are together. Let their memories and dreams be of each other. Whatever days they have left on this earth, let them spend it in each other's company. Thank you, Lord, for bringing them together at last."

After praying that heartfelt prayer, Beth just stood at the doorway, crying and looking at her brother and the love of his life now together. She stood there speechless for another thirty minutes. Though she was crying, she was also smiling; these were happy tears. Since Flutter had confided in her on many occasions of his love for Lily and his desire to be with her, only she knew of the significance of this moment—the Lord finally answered her brother's prayers.

As she left the hospital that night, Beth looked up at the sky and saw two shooting stars. Just as she was taking in this beautiful sight, she overheard a man and a woman talking about what they had seen.

"I always heard that when you see one shooting star that meant that a couple was communicating their love for one another," the man said.

"What does two shooting stars mean?" the woman asked.

"I don't know, but you can bet love is involved somehow."

Beth whispered to herself, "It means two people have finally found each other and are together now."

36

Over the next few months, nothing had changed with either Lily's or Flutter's physical condition. The doctors all said how amazed they were that even though there had been no changes, both patients were doing very well. One of the nurses even commented that she had witnessed both of them smiling at the same time during one of her hourly checks. "It was as though they were communicating with each other," she said. When Beth heard this, she knew that they were indeed communicating, and it was long overdue.

These few months when Flutter and Lily had found each other in a hospital room together had turned into two full years. The doctors were still not pleased with their lack of progress but were happy with their stable conditions. All seemed well with the couple in room 187 until a cold day in November.

The wind was blowing hard this day, and the weather anchors were telling everyone to "prepare for a hard wintry night with possible snow and sleet." People were stocking up on groceries and making sure that their firewood supplies were adequate.

Beth had decided to go and visit Lily and Flutter early this day in case she would not be able to get to the hospital in the next few days. Upon her arrival, she saw nurses and doctors running around in a hurried manner. She assumed there had been a medical emergency with one of the other patients.

When she approached the nurses' station, she heard a nurse say, "Room 187 stat." That was the room number she was headed to at that very moment. She began to run to the room, but when she got to the door, she noticed that the nurses and doctors were working on both Flutter and Lily.

"What happened? Will someone tell me what happened?" She kept repeating this over and over.

She was not able to see anything, and after what seemed like an eternity, she did not get the answer she was expecting. "Ma'am, would you please go to the waiting room and a doctor will be with you soon," one of the nurses said to her.

"What happened to them? What are you doing to them?"

"Ma'am, one of the doctors will be with you shortly."

Beth decided that she needed to call her nephews to let them know what was happening. She then did as the nurse had asked and waited (not so patiently) for the doctor to speak to her. In approximately twenty minutes, Flutter's children were at the hospital waiting with her to find out what was going on. What seemed like an eternity was really only about thirty minutes when, as promised, a doctor approached them with a solemn look on his face.

"Hello. Are any of you the family of Mr. Toliver?"

"Yes, Doctor, we are all his family," Beth replied.

"Great. My name is Dr. Cathcart, and I have been consulting with Dr. Larkin on Mr. Toliver's case during his stay here. It appears that your brother has started to come out of his coma—which is a good thing—but in that process, he had a stroke. The stroke has severely damaged his heart, and it does not look good. He may not make it through the night. He may not regain consciousness, but if he does, he will not be able to speak. I wanted to prepare you in the event that does happen. You can go see him now, if you like."

37

There was silence after the doctor spoke. Flutter's children were anxious to see their father, so they immediately went to his room.

"Doctor, I am also the only family Lily has. How is she?"

"Well, it is a medical oddity, to say the least. Mrs. Fields also started to come out of her coma tonight, and she too suffered a stroke. It is the strangest medical occurrence I have ever witnessed. Both of their monitors went off at exactly the same moment is what I'm told, and the staff worked on them at the same time for the same issues. My prognosis for her is the same, so when you go to see her, be prepared."

"All right, Dr. Cathcart. Thank you."

Beth sat down and just thought about what the doctor had said. She knew deep down that the two were planning their exits together, but she could not dare to tell anyone that. On the one hand, she was happy for them that they could finally be together; but on the other, their departure was going to be a sad time for all involved.

She finally got up and started her way to room 187. *Would this be the last time I'll see Flutter or Lily?* "Dad, when you get better and are able to get out of here, we're going fishing at our favorite fishing hole. Don't forget that you promised whoever caught the most fish, the other would cook them. So I expect that in a few months, we will be on the banks getting ready for you to cook," Richard told him.

All the other family members chimed in with their own comments to Flutter, but they did not pay any attention to Lily. Beth slowly walked into the room, walked over to Lily's bed, saw the tubes, and heard the beeping of the monitors that were keeping her alive. She held her hand and felt the warm limpness, but that did not stop her from holding on. She wanted to make sure that Lily knew she was not alone. While she was standing there, her thoughts went back to a conversation she had with Lily a few years ago.

Beth had gone by Lily's house right after her son and husband died to see how she was doing. They had become closer after her brother had confided in her about his true feelings for Lily. So when her family died, Beth took it upon herself to really get to know her and to comfort her. During this time, they became good friends. Her thoughts went back to one of those times she had stopped by her house to check up on her.

"Hi, Lily. I just stopped by to see if you want me to pick up something for you while I'm at the store."

"Hi, Beth. Thanks for stopping by. I think I have all that I need, but thank you anyway."

"What were you doing?"

"I was sitting here thinking about my life, my losses, and the fact that I am truly alone now. I know that I did not love my husband the way I should have, but I did love him nevertheless. Out of that love, we had a wonderful son. Now I have no husband and no son. When I think about how my life could have been different, I always think about Flutter. The love I felt and still feel for that man will go with me to the grave."

At this moment, Lily began to cry, and Beth consoled her with these words.

"Lily, I cannot tell you what the Lord had in store for you and my brother all those years ago. I do not understand why you lost your husband and son. But one thing I do know is that you are a child of the King, and he is always here with you. Don't question why you and Flutter could not be together on earth. Just remember that the Lord has a plan for us all, and we have to wait on him no matter what.

In Psalms 27:14 it says, 'Wait on the LORD: be of good courage, and he shall strengthen thine heart: wait, I say, on the LORD.' And he doesn't just say it once, he tells us two times to make sure we understand. So don't question the Lord or wonder what could have been. Just wait and see what the Lord has in store for you."

"You are right, Beth. I had a wonderful life with my husband and son, and I will always have those memories. No one can take that away from me."

The two smiled, hugged each other, and decided to have dinner together that night underneath the stars in Lily's backyard.

After having this brief moment of nostalgia, Beth came back to the reality of the timed beeps of the monitor indicating that her friend was still alive. As Beth continued to hold Lily's hand in a place that was not underneath the stars in a backyard, she smiled remembering the wonderful time they spent together. Those words she spoke to Lily all those years ago came to fruition, and she was sure that Lily knew that as well.

38

None of the doctors or staff members were able to tell any of the family any definitive information about what would happen next. So for several days, there was some family member keeping a vigilant watch at the bedside of their father. Beth made sure that Lily received the same careful watch when it was her turn to sleep in an uncomfortable hospital chair.

Flutter's family still had hope that their father would pull through this latest ordeal. Whenever they visited, there was laughter and lively conversation because they were sure he could hear them. However, on one of these laughter-filled visits, Flutter's breathing changed. His monitor went off, and the nurses and doctors hurriedly rushed into the room to see what needed to be done. While checking on Flutter as with the last time these monitors went off, Lily's monitors acted up in the same way, and another response team had to come into the room to check on her.

Both teams saw that both patients were leaving this world despite all their hard work to save them. Flutter's family was called which meant Lily would have family there as well with Beth. When they all arrived at the hospital, it seemed that Flutter and Lily felt that this was the opportune time to say their good-byes. There were tears, hugs, and held hands during this last farewell.

Beth made sure that Lily had the same farewell sentiments her brother was getting. She whispered in her hear only things that she and Flutter would understand, and she was sure that they both heard her word and agreed with everything she was saying.

"What a wonderful life you have both had on earth, and now what a wonderful life you will have in heaven together. I love both of you so much. If this is your time, then take it. We will miss you, but your happiness together will take away the pain I will feel without you here with me. God bless both of you," she whispered to both of them.

39

Love is patient, love is kind. It does not envy, it does not boast,
it is not proud. It does not dishonor others, it is not self-seeking,
it is not easily angered, it keeps no record of wrongs. Love does
not delight in evil but rejoices with the truth. It always protects,
always trusts, always hopes, always perseveres.

—1 Cor. 13:4–7 (NIV)

Oddly enough, their funerals were held exactly one week from the day they passed away and on the same day of the week, Saturday. Flutter's family wanted his service to be at 10:00 a.m. that morning while Lily's service was held at 1:00 p.m. Nobody but Beth understood the significance of this reality, but she knew in some way, each had a front seat at each other's service.

There were kind words said about them both, and many of the words were much of the same sentiment. They were good Christians, they both came from loving families, and both were wonderful people who'd had family members precede them in death. Not knowing at the time when the funeral plans were made with the respective preachers officiating each service, Flutter and Lily wanted the same song and scripture at their services. Both choirs softly sang their own revised versions of "I'll Fly Away" in the background as the minister read out loud the same scripture, Psalm 23.

Although the funerals were held in two different cities, strangely enough, they were buried in the same cemetery (Flutter had made sure that his children knew before their mother passed that he wanted to be buried in the Parwell Cemetery in a corner overlooking a small pond).

Flutter's family did not question their father's request not to be buried next to their mother. They just assumed that he wanted to be buried close to his parents in his hometown. Unknown to any of them, Lily had also given funeral and burial instructions to her close friend and sister Beth after her husband and son died. She too had made preparations to be buried in that same corner, overlooking the same small pond. Both of their wishes had been carried out exactly as they had instructed and without question.

In life Flutter and Lily never got together, but despite that difficulty, their love never died. Their true passions were never realized or acted upon, but those intense feelings were always there: the sweaty palms and heart palpitations were with Jeremy each time he saw his beloved, Lily, and Lily always had hopes that their love could and would be realized one day.

On each of their headstones were all the pertinent information, such as their names, birthdates, and dates of death. Also on each headstone were the words "*Not in life but in death.*" Neither Jeremy nor Lily knew they had both selected the same words that held such true meaning for both of them. More importantly, they both knew on some level that they would never be together in life. But now in death, Jeremy Bernard Toliver and Lily Marie Johnson were finally united that would last longer than matrimony. Buried next to each other were two star-crossed lovers. They were now together overlooking that pond in the "*Forever Love*" section of the cemetery.

As the days turned into months and the months into years, family and friends occasionally went to the Forever Love section of the cemetery to pay their respects to Jeremy or Lily. Neither family nor group of friends ever questioned the fact that they were buried side by side or that their headstone epitaphs were the same.

However, they all found it amazing and often commented on how the grass always seemed to stay green around the two separate headstones and how the purple wildflowers grew in abundance in this same area. It was as though they were informing everyone that they were together now and that they were happy. Not in life but in death, they were now able to be together.

Look for the next book from author R. Jay Berry beginning in 2016, *Forever Friends: Eight on Ten*. *Forever Friends: Eight on Ten* tells the true story of eight friends whose friendship transcended time.

Prologue

Do you remember what your life was like or what you were doing in the year 1976? Do you remember who the president or the vice president of the United States was then? As you think about your answers to these two questions, did your mind wander back in time and settle on a moment that had an impact on your life? Did you think about all the people you got to know in 1976 at school, at church, or at work?

If by any chance your thoughts rested on the people you met at a particular place of employment, did you smile or become so angry that you had to take a walk to bury the memories deep in your subconscious again? It may be safe to say that so many people could indeed relate to their very first work experience and the profound effect it had on their lives to this very day. It was not so much that these individuals were now earning their own keep in the world or the fact that they were now on Uncle Sam's tax roll that made them happy to be a part of the world of employment. Rather, it was the fact that they found other individuals they could relate to and had similar interests.

That is definitely the case for eight women who in 1976 became not just coworkers but also a close-knit family. It was not the job that sealed their bond but their love for one another.

These eight came from different backgrounds, ethnicities, neighborhoods, and age groups, but these differences did not matter to them. Their closeness was, of course, evident at work, but it brought them closer together after hours. Nothing was off limits—birthdays, holidays, concerts, weddings, divorces, childbirth, and, yes, even funerals were events that this group did not take for granted. One could say that these eight women loved each other unconditionally then and now.

Their story unfolds at the first meeting, and these eight women would become longtime friends, confidantes, and, most importantly, family.

Part I

Who Was Whom?

1

It was a cool rainy day in Deerman, Texas, where the lives of eight women were about to change. In this month, October; on this day, the first; and in this year, 1976. Whether it was for better or for worse, only time would tell.

It was orientation day for the recently employed members of an elite group of women who were to risk their safety and sanity every day. They had been hired as female officers to work on the tenth floor of the Deerman County Sheriff's Department, specifically with the female inmates. They all knew this was a dangerous assignment; but someone had to do it, so they thought, *Why not us?*

Many individuals had come through the doors of this sheriff's department in as many years, but many did not stay long enough to learn the ins and outs of law enforcement, let alone get to bond with their coworkers. However, this was not the case for eight women who not only learned the true meaning of keeping the peace but also how you come to depend on the people you work with.

"I need the following six individuals to meet Sgt. Ragland at the elevator to begin county orientation. Astor, Edwards, Goodman, Ogilvie, Simmons, and Woodson," announced the orientation commander.

Blank and bewildered looks were plastered on the faces of these women when they heard their names called. They all looked in the same direction at the same moment. Then the sergeant rose from her chair, positioned behind the county spokesperson, and walked toward the elevator. Her straight posture and steady, long strides showed that she was a confident woman.

She did not look at any of the women, but they all sensed that she was a no-nonsense person who would not tolerate shirking job responsibility by the quick manner in which they arose from their respective chairs to meet her at the elevator. None of the women recognized each other, but they slowly gathered at the elevator in anticipation.

The women ranged in ages from twenty two to thirty five, and just as varied as their ages were their heights—from five feet and three inches to five feet and eight inches (with their weights in proportion to them). Standing in silence, the women looked off into space, each trying not to look at each other; but unknown to any of them, their lives had already started to change.

No words were spoken as they all waited for the elevator door to open. All the women took quick glances at this woman they had not formally been introduced to yet. Her blank expression gave them no clue as to how she would interact with them.

The door slowly opened, and all the women entered the small room before the door had completely opened. Not a word was spoken as the sergeant pushed button number five. It took what seemed to be an eternity for the door to close and just as long for the elevator to move. When they finally reached their destination, the women waited for their appointed leader to take the first step onto the floor.

"Follow me, ladies" were Sgt. Ragland's first words to the group, and follow her was what they did.

Sgt. Ragland was an Anglo woman who was approximately five feet and six inches tall and weighed about a hundred and sixty pounds. She was one of the first three women to not only be hired to work as a matron at the county, but most importantly, she was also the first woman to be promoted to her current rank. She was put in charge of working on the tenth floor, where the female prisoners were housed.

Sgt. Ragland excelled at her job as well as in training new recruits. What the ladies were soon to find out was that all the officers at the sheriff's department, especially the female officers, looked up to her because of her dedication to her job, her title, and the training she provided for her female trainees.

This was day one of many days together for these unsuspecting fledglings who would one day fly on their own at the Deerman County Sheriff's Department.

HD
NW

CPSIA information can be obtained at www.ICGtesting.com
Printed in the USA
LVOW10s0855190816

500674LV00018B/113/P